MANY KINDS OF MAGIC

Other children's books by the author

Boori
Darkness Under the Hills
Shadows Among the Leaves
Following the Gold

BILL SCOTT

MANY KINDS OF MAGIC

VIKING

assisted by the Literature Board
of the Australia Council

Poo831 95321

Viking
Penguin Books Australia Ltd
487 Maroondah Highway, PO Box 257
Ringwood, Victoria, 3134, Australia
Penguin Books Ltd
Harmondsworth, Middlesex, England
Viking Penguin Inc.
40 West 23rd Street, New York, NY 10010, USA
Penguin Books Canada Limited
2801 John Street, Markham, Ontario, Canada, L3R 1B4
Penguin Books (N.Z.) Ltd
182-190 Wairau Road, Auckland 10, New Zealand

First published by Viking, 1990

Typeset in Goudy by Midland Typesetters, Maryborough, Victoria
Made and printed by Australian Print Group, Maryborough, Victoria

CIP

Scott, Bill, 1923-
Many kinds of magic.

ISBN 0670829714.

1. Tales—Juvenile literature. I. Title.

398.2

Creative writing program assisted by the Australia Council,
the Federal Government's arts funding and advisory body.

CONTENTS

BAMBOO BASKET BOY

A long time ago in Japan there was a young man who wanted to be a painter. He lived in a tiny hut in the mountains. Up high there were no farms; only great rocks and stony precipices, bare mountain peaks, steep hillsides covered with pine and fir trees, and enormous thickets of bamboo. From Spring until Autumn a stream of melted snow-water tumbled and sang in its rocky bed close by his front door.

He was an orphan. His parents had died when he was only thirteen years old. His father had cleared some ground of rocks, and levelled it enough to grow some few vegetables in the Summer but it was not enough to support the little family. They made their living with the help of the generous bamboo thicket. During the day they cut long green and golden canes and carried them back to the hut, and by firelight in the evenings they wove them into baskets and other useful things.

After his parents died the youth continued to live in the hut. Once a month he would take a great bundle of baskets on his back

1

and walk the long distance to the nearest market town. There he would sell them to buy dried fish and rice to eat in the month ahead. He always went on the day of the full moon because the way was so long and hard that he could not get home in daylight. He needed the soft moonlight to guide him before he got back to his home. The people at the market called him Bamboo Basket Boy.

He made fine, strong baskets that people were eager to buy, but this was not what he really wanted to do. His mother and father had taught him his letters, and the brushes and ink were still in the hut. When he had finished work for the day, especially when the snow lay thick in Winter and he did not have to tend the garden, he would take the brushes and ink-stone from the box where he kept them and try to paint the things he knew so well. He drew tall bamboo stems, and fir trees and rocks half-hidden in the mist that sometimes filled the valley. He painted the fish that swam in the clear stream, birds that sang in the forest, and deer he saw on the high slopes. He worked and worked at his painting, patiently drawing and re-drawing, but he was never satisfied with his pictures.

One day when he was at the market, weary from his long walk and heavy burden, one of the merchants said to him, 'Hey! Bamboo Basket Boy, there is a famous painter from the capital staying at the inn! He is making a pilgrimage to the Shrines, and he will stay for a few days. You are a painter too, why don't you go and have a talk with him!' He knew the man was laughing at him, yet when he had sold his baskets he went to the inn and enquired for the painter. At first the inn-keeper would not let him in, but he pleaded so hard that at last a servant took him to where the thin old man was drinking tea in the garden.

The old artist was not put off by the boy's rough clothes and manners. He asked the youth in a kindly way what he wanted.

'I want to be a painter, Sensei,' said the young man. 'I try hard, but what I achieve does not satisfy me at all.'

The old man handed him a brush and a sheet of paper. 'Paint!' he said sharply. Bamboo Basket Boy took the brush and drew a fish in a stream. The other guests murmured in surprise that a country-bred, inelegant young fellow should have such skill but the old man was not impressed. He looked severely at the boy.

'Your fish does not swim!' he said.

The youth nodded and tears filled his eyes.

The old master took up the brush in his turn. He ground fresh ink and mixed it to his satisfaction. Then he took a fresh sheet of paper and closed his eyes for a moment. When he opened them he dipped the brush, and in a few swift, sweeping strokes drew a fish. It was done in a second, yet all gasped with amazement. The carp he drew seemed to swim strongly up the page. 'My fish swims and breathes, young man,' he said.

The basket-maker nodded dumbly, and when his emotion let him speak he said sadly, 'That is what I mean. That is what I cannot do.'

The old man took a fresh sheet of paper and once more closed his eyes in concentration. All grew hushed. He suddenly opened his eyes and with a few lightning strokes, there was the face of Bamboo Basket Boy drawn with such skill and understanding that his unhappiness seemed to cry aloud.

'That is how you feel,' said the old man.

'Sensei, will you take me to be your servant? I will carry your luggage, I will sweep your house and tend your garden.'

'I have no money to pay you,' said the old man, looking intently at the youth.

'I want no money, only that you teach me,' cried the lad.

The old man did not answer him, only picked up a brick that lay at his feet and began to rub it upon a stone.

'What are you doing?' asked a rich merchant who sat nearby.

'I am making a mirror out of this brick. See, I'm polishing it!' said the old man.

'But you cannot make a mirror from mud!' cried the astounded man.

'Perhaps mud can turn itself into a mirror if it tries,' said the old painter. 'Listen, boy. Go home to your mountain. Think very hard about what you want most to do in the world. When Winter is gone, if you still wish to learn, come to my house in Kyoto and I will find out if you are metal or mud. You may become a mirror after all; but if you are clay then no amount of polishing by me will turn you into one.'

Bamboo Basket Boy bowed his farewells and went sadly back to the market-place. He bought his food for the coming month and tied it to his bamboo backpack. He still had a little money left, for he had

Many Kinds of Magic

got good prices for his wares. As he left the market to go home he passed the booth of the wine-seller. Some men outside were drinking together and singing:

Honourable Spirit of Rice!
When we drink Your essence
Sadness flies away like a wild bird,
Joy and laughter come in with you!

They sounded very happy, so the youth went to the dealer and said, 'Give me a large jar of wine to take home with me to the mountains.' The merchant sold him a large jar of wine. He hung it from the carrying-frame on his back then began to hurry home because he had stayed much later than usual in the town.

Night had fallen and the moon had raised his great golden lamp by the time the lad reached the faint path that led into the forest. He strode along, still quiet and thoughtful, unhappy and unsettled in his mind, undecided about what he should do when the end of Winter came. The jar of wine clinked musically in time with his steps as he climbed the steep path among the tall forest trees. He was startled from his musing by a voice calling him.

'Hey! Brother! Wait for me!' called the voice.

Looking back downhill he saw a very sturdy little man hastening after him. 'Who are you, Brother, and what do you want?' he asked. The stranger caught up with him, and in the moonlight could be seen quite clearly. 'I am going to a party to view the moonlight on the tops of the forest trees,' said the sturdy little man. 'I see you have wine with you. If you care to bring it along you would be very welcome at the party. There will be music and dancing and a feast; merry companionship, and bright light from the Lantern of Tsukinomi!'

Bamboo Basket Boy suddenly lost all his sorrow and a spirit of recklessness filled his heart. He said, 'Hard Winter comes, snow on the pines; ice on the waterfall, earth all frozen. Let us be joyful, music and drinking.'

The sturdy man clapped his hands for joy and led him swiftly to a clearing in the forest. It was on top of a hill, and all around was a great gathering of little men. They had piles of food and heaps of wine-jars. Some played on bamboo flutes, some beat time, and others danced in a circle, singing. A sweet scent of flowers filled the air and a sharp smell of herbs crushed by their dancing feet filled his nostrils. He lay his burden on the ground, and for the first time in his life he drank wine. It went to his head and soon he began dancing and singing with the best of them.

> *Yama no Kami! Spirits of the mountains,*
> *See, we are dancing, hear, we are singing*
> *Under the light of Tsukinomi's lantern!*

he sang, dancing in a circle and waving his arms like a fir tree in a great wind.

Suddenly he realized that all the others had fallen silent and that he was singing and dancing alone. They were standing round in a circle beating time to his song by thumping their sinewy hands on their hard, round bellies. 'PON-poko-pon-pon. PON-poko-pon-pon.' He was too elated to be frightened by now; though he realized that these were not men at all, but badgers. Badgers are cheerful animals. They love music and dancing and drinking, and here he was at one of their parties! He sang louder and louder and the little men drummed along with him till they all burst out laughing with joy and exhaustion and sat down to have more food and another drink.

Bamboo Basket Boy found himself sitting next to the biggest badger, a little apart from all the others. The wine was working in his brain by now and he found himself telling the thickset little man about wanting to be a painter and the old man's invitation to go to Kyoto and be his servant.

The badger listened in silence, then said, 'What do *you* really want to do?'

'I don't know,' admitted the lad. 'You see, I love the mountains and the animals; the long silence of the snow in Winter, the green joy of Spring when buds break from the black wood and the plum and cherry trees adorn themselves with blossom. I love the heavy warmth of Summer and the smell of wood-smoke on the chill, blue evenings of Autumn such as we have with us now. Yet, Tanuki-san, it is a hard life and now a hard choice. I want to be a painter – to be able to paint a fish that swims and moves like the carp of the old man! You are older and wiser than me. Honourably advise me, please.'

The badger thought for a while, then said, 'The things you love most about the mountains are all peaceful things. Yet there is no peace unless there is peace in the heart. You must go to Kyoto, of course. If, after a time, the fish you paint still stays only a painting of a fish then you can come back to the mountains and be a basket-maker again. We badgers will look after your hut for you in case you do come back.'

Bamboo Basket Boy wept a little then, but he was comforted by what Badger had said. After a little while he cheered up and drank and sang some more. Then all the wine he had drunk began to affect his legs and his senses and the badgers had to help him home when the party was over.

When he woke late next morning his head ached abominably and his stomach was sick inside from the wine, and sore outside where he had been beating it like a badger. He felt terribly ill, and swore he would never drink so much again. Instead he worked as hard as he could for the rest of Autumn. By the time the first snow fell, when he could no longer go safely to the thicket for bamboo, he had cut and stored a great pile; enough to let him work in the hut for the whole Winter.

When Spring came his house was almost filled with baskets so he had to make four trips down to the market before all were sold. On the last journey back to the hut he bought another large jar of wine, the largest one he could carry, and took it home with him.

Early next morning he rose and scrubbed his hut till it shone. He tidied everything away and pulled all the weeds from his little garden. When all was ready, he took the wine to the top of the hill where the party had been and called aloud many times. At last he saw a stirring in the bushes at the edge of the clearing and was delighted to see the strong jaws, the white mask and great eyes of a huge badger looking at him.

He bowed and said, 'Honourable friend, I am about to go to Kyoto to find the old man. I have brought you a parting gift.'

The badger came from the undergrowth. It wore a lotus leaf on its head for a hat, and a long cloak covering its body, sheltering it from the sharp Spring wind. It said, 'Remember, if you are not happy and successful in your search, your friends will wait impatiently here for your return. We will look after your home as we promised. Now, here is a gift for you.' It plucked a small tuft of fur from its body and gave this to Bamboo Basket Boy. 'If you make brushes from this fur they may help you, for I have Magic and some of that magic is in every part of me. I think you will need it some day, a very long time from now, so don't go wasting it or using it foolishly. Thank you for the gift you have brought us, and remember your friends in the mountains when you are far away.'

The badger picked up the wine jar, which was almost as tall as itself, and tottered away with it into the cover of the bushes. The youth returned to his hut, took up his small bundle of belongings and set off downhill on the long road to the capital.

In Kyoto a strange new life began for him. He rose before sunrise and worked hard in his master's garden. He prepared breakfast for the old man and took it to him. While the old gentleman sat and drank tea in his small, elegant garden the boy cleaned the house and did the marketing. When all was completed he would go to the little studio where his master worked, to try to learn. Gradually his control of the brush improved, but still he could not breathe life into his paintings as his master could.

When Summer was over and the maple leaves began turning crimson and scarlet like hot fires against the cool, blue mist of Autumn evenings, the old man said to him, 'You must put away your brush for a time. Now we find out whether you are made from metal or clay! All Winter, when you have spare time from your duties, you must sit quite still and alone and think about this poem. When you are sure you know what it means, come and tell me.'

He handed the young man a poem, written beautifully in large characters on a scroll of purest silk. The poem said:

> Rain, hail, snow,
> Ice as well, are set apart from each other.
> But when they melt –
> All are the same water
> Running over the rocks
> In the valley stream.

The student bowed and retired to his little room, where he hung the scroll reverently in the alcove near his sleeping-mat. When he was not busy with his work he would kneel before the alcove and consider the poem until it sang in his heart. All winter he looked and thought, and by the time the first plum-blossom burst from the boughs he thought he knew something about what the old man meant him to learn.

The spirit of things took many forms as did the water but really it remained the same though it seemed different! It was the task of the artist to consider the water as well as the forms it could take. Now he understood why the master closed his eyes before making a painting. He was contemplating the spirit of the thing he was about to draw! The youth drew his brush from its case and with stiff fingers (for he had not touched it since Autumn), he drew a fish in a stream. Though the lines were not so elegant as when he was constantly practising, yet his fish grew clear on the paper. It sprang from his spirit, ran down his arm and through the bristles of the brush, and suddenly, quickly, it swam on to the page before him!

Taking the drawing in his suddenly shaking hands he ran to the door of his master's room. Then he took hold upon his undignified excitement, and when he had entered and bowed, he silently extended the page to the old man. The old man looked at it for a moment, then smiled at him.

' "The moon reflected in the stream, the wind in the fir trees – This breath flows through me, and through my son also," ' he quoted. Then he bowed to the boy in his turn, and said, 'This fish swims, and you are metal, not clay. Welcome.'

After this the old master taught him many things. When the master died a few years later he left his small house and garden and his money to the young man, who by this time was fully grown and becoming famous. Still he would not charge large sums for his work, and people thought him foolish, but he only smiled and continued to work hard teaching himself to paint even better. So the years went by, and his fame and reputation grew until he was counted to be among the finest artists of his time.

Then great turmoil and trouble came to the land. Men strove with each other for power. Battles were fought and much blood was spilled as war lords fought, army against army. Tears were on the cheeks of many, and some thought the world would end, so tremendous was the struggle. The artist who had once been Bamboo Basket Boy, who was now old and alone (for his servants had been taken to be soldiers), remembered a little hut in the mountains. There was talk that war would even come to the capital, so he dressed simply in a plain robe, took a little money and some food, and walked away from his house without even looking back at it. He set off for the mountains, and in two weeks was walking slowly up the old path to the hut, carrying dried fish and rice in two baskets slung on a pole he bore across his shoulders.

When he reached his old home he was delighted to find it swept and scrubbed and clean as he had left it. Even the garden plot had been weeded! 'Faithful friends!' he said. 'You have kept your word, even though you must have despaired that I would ever return.'

Quietly he settled in to the house again, planted his garden and mended or replaced the few things that had rotted or broken in the winter storms. Then began a quiet life once more. Sometimes he collected fire-wood, sometimes he cultivated his garden, sometimes he painted the fish in the stream and the animals of the forest, sometimes the rocks half-hidden in the mist of twilight. The paintings glowed and breathed life as he hung them around the walls of his simple dwelling.

Once a month, at the time of the full moon, he would take some of them to the market town and sell them. He no longer tried to return on the same day, however. He would stay at the inn overnight, and next morning hire a porter to carry the bundles for him to the place where the faint track left the main highway. Though he did not ask for much money for his paintings, yet his reputation grew among those who know of such things. They did not know he was the famous master from Kyoto, for he never told anyone, and so they called him The Master Of The Bamboo Grove.

Each month he bought a large jar of wine from the booth of the merchant and took it to the hilltop where he had danced and sung so many years ago. There he left it and although he never saw anyone there, each month he would find the jar empty and washed clean ready to be replaced by a full one. He did this for the badgers in thanks and gratitude for the care and love they had showed him by looking after his house for so many years.

Meanwhile, in the great world outside the lonely mountains one war lord had become supreme. He decided that the new capital would no longer be at Kyoto, but would be removed to Yedo. He caused great palaces and a fortress to be built for himself, his soldiers and family and retainers. When his new palace was complete he called his Steward and asked: 'How shall we make this new palace more beautiful than any other building in the whole of the land of Japan?'

'Lord, send for the most skilled in their arts to come here and make pottery and sculptures, paintings and statues, inscriptions on stone and metal, clothes and hangings of the greatest magnificence,' said the Steward.

'Let it be proclaimed thus,' said the Shogun.

Artists, craftsmen and skilled needle-women were brought from all over the land. They worked for years to beautify the new palace. Clever gardeners formed and tended beautiful gardens and planted many trees; lakes were formed and streams diverted, until the people said no palace had ever been built that was more lovely. Those who thought otherwise very sensibly did not say so, for to criticise the works of the Shogun meant instant death.

The Steward came to the Shogun one day and said, 'There is a painter called Master Of The Bamboo Grove who did not come when we summoned him. He says he is too old and frail to make such a long journey, and begs to be excused.'

'Send soldiers to bring him here!' said the Shogun, and they did.

When the old man was brought to Yedo the Steward said to him, 'Because you have disobeyed, the master says this: old Bamboo Man must paint the most beautiful scene in the world on the walls of the Audience Chamber. If it is inferior, then you must be slain.'

The old man bowed his head in submission. He took the tools of his trade and began work as he had been instructed. Word soon passed around among the other artists that the most wonderful thing was being created on the wall of the audience chamber.

One by one and two by two they came to see and all were awed by the beauty of the scene that was being painted. It was the picture of a simple hut in the mountains with a small garden behind it. It overlooked a flowing stream among rough rocks, painted so well you could almost hear the sound of the freshets of water. It was surrounded by steep slopes of pine and fir trees and graceful animals peered from among the great trunks. Brilliant birds flew through the air and seemed to hover on the walls. In the foreground was an enormous bamboo thicket that stirred and swayed forever in an unseen wind. From among the bamboos peered the head of a badger.

The other painters shook their heads in despair of ever accomplishing such a picture themselves and one of them told the Steward that this old man was making the greatest picture that ever had been drawn for the pleasure of the Shogun.

'When it is complete it will be the greatest picture in the world,' he said. 'Your Master will have the best painting of all times.'

The Steward told this to the Shogun. His cruel master then said, 'As soon as the old man has finished the picture, kill him!'

The Steward exclaimed in horror, but the Shogun explained, 'If we reward him and let him go free he might paint an even better picture for someone else! Therefore he must die, but be sure he finishes the picture first!'

After that there were always two soldiers with bows

stationed in the Audience Chamber while the old Bamboo Master worked at his painting. Being very wise, he knew quite well what was in the mind of the Shogun but he was calm. He worked on until, one evening, it was complete save for some details on the hut wall. As the light faded and he could not see any longer to work, he said to one of the soldiers, 'Tomorrow I will finish.' The soldier reported this to the Steward and he in turn told his master.

'I will come and watch the end,' said the warlord.

In the quiet of his little chamber that night the old painter unrolled a small piece of faded silk containing some badger hair. He took it and carefully made from it a brush, such a clever brush! Next morning when he went to finish the painting he found the Shogun there with his generals and followers, ranked upon the floor to see the end of his painting and his life. The old man bowed expressionlessly and began work, using the new brush he had made. He painted a window upon the blank wall of the little hut. It was a most beautiful window, with a warm light upon the oiled paper glazing as though a fire flickered inside the little building. The old man painted the finishing touches.

When it was complete the Shogun raised his hand and the soldiers bent their bows and waited for him to drop his arm. The old Master Of The Bamboo Grove bowed again to the Shogun, and turned to the painting. Then something happened for which no one was prepared. The old man smoothly opened the painted window, scrambled through it, and closed it again from the other side! The onlookers knelt, frozen with astonishment. Then all was uproar, and everyone hastened to search for the old painter, but although they turned the whole palace and town upside down looking for him, no trace could be found. When they looked closely again at the painting, they were astonished to find that the badger head no longer peeped from the bamboo clump. It seemed as though it, too, had gone forever.

Soldiers were sent to the hut on the mountainside where they had originally arrested the old man. Though they sometimes seemed to be able to see it from the opposite side of the valley, when they reached the place it was never there! After some time they gave up and returned to the capital, leaving the mountain valley as peaceful and deserted as it had always been. The old man was never seen again.

However, farmers who sometimes go to the high slopes to collect dead branches for firewood for the Winter tell a strange story, and none will sleep in that valley at night. They say that at the time of the full moon, especially the full moon of August, they hear the sound of many voices singing on a nearby hilltop. Sometimes they hear the voice of a very old man singing alone:

> *Yama no Kami! Spirits of the mountains,*
> *See, we are dancing, hear, we are singing*
> *Under the light of Tsukinomi's Lantern!*

while all around the hillsides echo the sound of many little drums playing, 'PON-poko-pon-pon. PON-poko-pon-pon, PON-poko-pon-pon!'

JAKAMARRA

Jakamarra lived with his people away out in the middle of the Great Australian Loneliness. He was a young man and a good dancer. He needed red ochre to grind to powder on a stone so he could make paint to paint the patterns on his body for the dance at the night of the full moon. Red ochre was scarce and precious. It came such a long way across the desert before it reached his people. Jakamarra had none because he was a young man but his grandfather had some. So he went to the old man, and Bush Flies went with him. They always did! 'Grandfather, grandfather, I need red ochre to paint the marks on my body for the dance. Please give me some!'

The old man was sitting in a shady place carving fine patterns on a spear-thrower with a chip of flint. He looked at the young man standing before him with proud head and shining skin.

He said, 'So, you want a bit of ochre, do you? I only seem to see you when you want something. You haven't brought me a present of honey for a long time, have you?

You know how I love honey! Maybe if a young man brought me some honey I could find red ochre. I wouldn't promise, but I could have a look to see if there was any left.'

'Perhaps you might like to give me some ochre now and I could bring the honey another time,' said Jakamarra hopefully.

The old man smiled and silently went on carving.

'Where am I going to find honey at this dry time of year?' asked Jakamarra in despair. Grandfather went on carving, and after a time he said, without looking up, 'Perhaps Bee might give you some if you asked politely. Now leave me in peace. This is a tricky bit. I'll talk to you again when I have something sweet to eat!'

Jakamarra stayed arguing but it was no use. The old man didn't give any sign he heard him. Presently the youth sighed and walked away. No good trying to argue with Grandfather when he got stubborn like that. Better go and try to find some honey!

Jakamarra went to the secret waterhole of his people. Bush Flies went with him. They always did. He sat on a rounded boulder near the crack where you slipped in the hollow tube of cane-grass to suck up the water, and waited. Soon a stingless native bee came secretly and quietly from the crack in the stone. He caught it gently in his palm and stuck a little tuft of white fluff from the wild cotton-bush to its belly. Then he let it go and ran after its wavering flight; keeping one eye on the flash of white in the bright sunlight and the other eye on the ground so he wouldn't trip over stones or fallen trees. He was panting like a lizard in the heat by the time he saw the little clump of straggly trees where the bee was going. Then he slowed and walked. So did Bush Flies.

When he reached the clump he was delighted to find that one of the shrubs was flowering. He waited by the blossoms until another bee came along, gathering pollen from the flowerets. He watched it with his keen eyes in the patchy sunlight that flickered through the leaves, and saw it fly off to a ghost gum that raised its green leaves above the snowy-powdered trunk. He followed and was delighted to find a little hole in one branch that was stained red and brown from *something* that hid inside. He sat on the ground near the hole and called softly:

> *Bee, Bee,*
> *Please give me some honey for my Grandfather*
> *So he will give me some red ochre*
> *So I can paint myself for the dance at the full*
>   *moon.*

When Jakamarra had sung this three times he thought he heard a mumbling, dim voice from inside the branch. It seemed to say, 'This is the dry time. I need the honey to feed the babies so they will grow strong to find honey to feed the babies so they will grow strong to find honey to feed the babies so they will . . .'

It would probably have gone on a lot longer but Jakamarra interrupted rudely. 'But I *need* the honey. Is there something you would like that you would exchange for some honeycomb?'

The voice hummed wordlessly for a while, then it said, 'The water is too far away. If you can get Rain

Spirit to fill the empty waterhole so we can get water easily, then we wouldn't have to fly so far to get water to become strong to get honey to feed the babies so they will grow strong to find honey to feed the babies so they will grow strong . . .'

'*All right*! You said that before. Will you really give me some honey if I get you the water?'

'Yes, I think I might,' said Bee.

'Then I'll go and see Rain Spirit,' said Jakamarra and off he went. Bush Flies went with him. They always did.

He walked and trotted and ran and walked again until he came to the rocky mountain where Rain Spirit lived. Rain Spirit was a huge brown frog. Every year when the Wet was over she would hop and spring around drinking up as much as she could hold to keep the water safe until the next Time of Rain. When her body was so full that it squelched and bulged as she leapt along she would come to the mountain and squat among the rocks like a warty boulder until the wet winds came again from the north and the Old Men told her to set the waters free. All through the Dry Time the only way to get a bit of water from her was to make her laugh. This was hard to do because she didn't find many things funny! Jakamarra knew he would have a hard time with her!

When he reached the foot of the mountain and stood in front of her face he looked like a little Bush Fly in front of a boulder. He shouted:

Rain Spirit, Rain Spirit, please fill Bee's waterhole

> So Bee will give me some honey for Grand-
> father
> So Grandfather will give me some red ochre
> So I can paint myself for the dance at the full
> moon.

Rain Spirit opened one eye, big and golden as the full moon when it first rises, and looked at Jakamarra. Then she closed it again and shook her head so firmly that boulders rolled down the slope and Jakamarra had to dodge quickly to save his poor toes from being squashed.

'Then I will *make* you laugh!' said Jakamarra.

He danced, he capered, he pulled faces, he sang silly songs, he told funny stories and recited funny poems till the trees split their bark laughing, the little skinks roared with mirth and the willy-willies spun in happiness round and round on the white clay-pan at the foot of the steep slopes. All Rain Spirit did was to open tiny slits between her eyelids like strips of golden light and she kept her mouth firmly shut. Jakamarra collapsed under a desert oak tree in the shade while the sweat trickled down his cheeks and the millions of Bush Flies landed on him and begged him to go on being funny! But he was too weary. Then he heard a harsh laugh from the crown of drooping branches. Looking up he saw Galah in his smart suit with a pearl-grey coat and bright pink trousers, looking down at him with head tilted to one side.

'AAAAARRKK! You'll never make her laugh like that. AAAAWWKK! You have to tickle her, and there's only one thing to tickle her with.

CAAARRRRRKK! Go to Big Lake and get a feather from Old Pelican! AAARRRRGH! Tickle her under the chin with that and she'll LARRRRRFF!' Jakamarra got slowly to his feet and set off again, this time for the Big Lake. Bush Flies went with him. They always do.

Big Lake was a long way off. Most Dry Times it wasn't a lake at all, just endless kilometres of salty mud; but this year it was full of water. Pelican with his wives and children and grandchildren and great-grandchildren and their friends, relatives and acquaintances had gathered at the lake. They were all busy fishing and building nests and raising families and exchanging the gossip from Cape York and Bass Strait and the Kimberleys and Cape Leeuwin. You can't imagine the noise that was going on! Babies were crying, men were shouting and singing and boasting about their fishing, wives were gossiping with friends and neighbours, and even those who couldn't find anyone to talk to were talking to themselves! Jakamarra could hear them when he was still kilometres away.

When he arrived at their enormous camp he found there was such a huge mob of them that it was almost impossible to discover who was the real Old Pelican among all the rest. But at last he was directed to a very Old Bird who was sitting by himself, muttering. His black feathers were rusty with age, and his white feathers were brown with mud and he had bits of old fish stuck to his chest because he was a sloppy eater.

Jakamarra saluted him and said:

Many Kinds of Magic

Old Pelican, Old Pelican, please give me a
feather from your wing,
So I can tickle Rain Spirit under the chin so she
laughs,
So the water runs and fills Bee's waterhole,
So Bee will give me some honey for Grandfather
So Grandfather will give me some red ochre
So I can paint myself for the dance at the full
moon.

'Speak up! Speak up! I'm a bit deaf, and this lot make such a noise! Listen to those two over there bragging about the fish they caught yesterday! You should just have seen the one I nearly got the day before yesterday! It was *this* big!' Old Pelican stretched his wide wings as far as they would go and Jakamarra gasped in amazement. Also in doubt, for he didn't quite believe Pelican but he knew that fishermen like you to believe their stories.

He whistled in surprise, and said, 'Please may I have a feather from your wing?' (He didn't want to have to say it all again, and he was a little breathless from travelling so far and shouting so loudly above the noise the other birds were making.)

'Feather? Feather? You can see yourself I haven't got enough left to go throwing any away! I need every one I have to go fishing. No, I won't give you any feather, indeed I won't! Unless . . .'

His voice tailed off and he got a cunning look in his tiny, round, black, beady eye.

'Unless what?' asked Jakamarra dismally.

'Oh, don't worry yourself! You'd never find him

anyway! I've tried often enough, and I can't,' said Old Pelican, watching Jakamarra out of the corner of his left eye.

'Find who?'

'Old Wallaroo. He borrowed my club a long time ago and he hasn't brought it back.'

'Why don't you ask him for it, then?'

'I can't find him. You know what *he* looks like. So thick and humpy and brown! When he sits still he looks *exactly* like those brown rocks on the hill where he lives. I've looked and looked and I can't ever see him.'

'I'll make you a new club if you like, and if you will give me a feather for it.'

'I don't want a new one!' shouted Old Pelican. 'I want my very own club back! You find him and bring it back to me and I'll give you a feather. You can't ask fairer than that.'

'Oh, all right!' groaned Jakamarra. 'I'll get your club back.' He set off for the hills where Wallaroo lived. Bush Flies went with him, of course. They always do.

When he got there at last he was so tired he just climbed the nearest hill and squatted in the shade to rest. He sat quite still, not stirring, just looking out over the brown plains where the heat-waves danced with the whirlwinds, and listened to the dry, brown leaves rattle on the thin branches overhead as they were stirred by the eternal wind that blows over the endless plains.

After a while he blinked and stared. What he had thought to be another big boulder standing nearby had changed shape. He looked but nothing more happened. Then suddenly he saw that it wasn't a boulder at all! It was Old Man Wallaroo, sitting on his tail and peering at him. Jakamarra laughed.

'I see you, I see you!' he shouted 'It's no use hiding there. I'm looking for you and I've found you. What have you done with Pelican's club? He sent me to get it back from you. He wants it. You've had it too long, you know; you should have taken it back long ago.'

Wallaroo shuffled his long thick feet in the red sand. 'Why are you running errands for that lazy old man?' he asked.

> *Wallaroo, Wallaroo, give me the club*
> *So I can take it to Old Man Pelican*
> *So he will give me a feather from his wing,*
> *So I can tickle Rain Spirit under the chin so she*
> *   laughs*
> *So the water runs and fills Bee's waterhole*
> *So Bee will give me some honey for Grand-*
> *   father,*
> *So Grandfather will give me some red ochre*
> *So I can paint myself for the dance at the full*
> *   moon,*

sang Jakamarra.

'I beg your pardon?' said Wallaroo, bewildered.

'I'm not going to say all that again,' said Jakamarra. 'Just give me the club and I'll go away.'

Wallaroo looked embarrassed. 'Actually, I haven't got it just now. Honey Ant asked for a loan of it, and I lent it to him. He hasn't brought it back. Maybe if you went there and asked him for it, he would bring it back and then I could give it to you. I'd go myself only I have a sore foot!' (He hadn't really got a sore foot; to tell the truth he was ashamed of himself for not bringing the club back sooner.)

'Well, where has Honey Ant got his tunnels these days?'

'On the saltbush flat near the mountain where men get stones to make axe-heads,' said Wallaroo.

'Then I suppose I'd better go and see Honey Ant.'

Jakamarra ran again through the plains of saltbush and spinifex and came to the mountain. Bush Flies went with him, they always do. Jakamarra looked and studied and studied and looked and after studying and looking for hours he found the tiny hole in the ground where Honey Ant had his front door. He lay down close to the hole and whispered in his very tiniest voice down the hole:

> *Honey Ant, Honey Ant, please give me the club you borrowed*
> *So I can take it to Wallaroo, so he will give it to Pelican,*
> *So Pelican will give me a feather from his wing*
> *So I can tickle Rain Spirit under the chin and make her laugh*
> *So the water runs and fills Bee's waterhole*
> *So Bee will give me some honey for Grandfather,*
> *So Grandfather will give me some red ochre*
> *So I can paint myself for the dance at full moon.*

When he had finished the song, which by now was

Many Kinds of Magic

quite long, he lay on his side and placed his ear close to the hole. He heard a faint rustling underground like someone tearing paper-bark then a little, whispery voice said: 'We will give it back to him if you will get Marsupial Mole to promise not to dig around our home any more. He burrows through our dining room and cookhouse and bedroom and nursery so the walls fall in and we have to dig them all out again. Do that for us and we will give the club back to Wallaroo.'

'Where is Marsupial Mole these days? It's hard to find someone who lives under the sand all the time!'

'Over toward the Tanami, you'll find him easy enough,' said the whispery voice. 'He follows us around. Try going along our back trail and he'll be there, snuffling and scraping.'

Off through the sandhills and blue bush and past the ghost-gums ran Jakamarra with Bush Flies still following. When he got to the big sand ridges he found Marsupial Mole sooner than he expected.

It was always difficult to talk to Marsupial Mole. He had no eyes so you couldn't tell whether he was awake or asleep. He had no ears though he could hear if you shouted very loud at the right and proper end of him. You could tell which was his front end by seeing which way his feet were pointing. Jakamarra took a good look, then knelt beside the little golden creature and shouted loudly:

> Mole, Mole,
> Please stop digging through Honey Ant's
>   houses

So Honey Ant will give Wallaroo the Pelican's
  club,
So Wallaroo can give it to me,
So I can give it to Pelican,
So Pelican can give me a feather from his wing
So I can tickle Rain Spirit under the chin and
  make her laugh,
So the water runs and fills Bee's waterhole,
So Bee will give me some honey for Grand-
  father
So Grandfather will give me some red ochre
So I can paint myself for the dance at the full
  moon.

Mole muttered and mumbled and grizzled and grumbled and at last said, 'The sand. The sand gets under my skin. The sand gets under my skin when I'm burrowing through it and it itches. Itches. It tickles and scratches and grinds and rasps so much I can't understand what you are whispering about. If you'll just unbutton my moleskin jacket and give it a good shake-out . . . The buttons are all along the top of my back where I can't reach. Silly. Silly place. Silly place to put your buttons, where you can't reach them. Oh, I do need a good brush-down and scrub-up. Then I'll be able to hear what you're saying.'

Jakamarra began the difficult job of finding all the buttons along Mole's backbone. When he had gently and carefully undone them all, he eased the beautiful golden fur jacket over Mole's belly and shoulders and arms and legs until Mole could step out of it. Then he turned it inside out, right down to the tiniest claw-tip and gave it a good shaking while Mole stood and

Many Kinds of Magic

shivered despite the heat; and giggled and spluttered and chuckled while Bush Flies walked and tickled all over his bare pink body, as Bush Flies always do.

When he was sure all the sand was out of the skin, Jakamarra turned it right side out. Mole struggled and squeezed and said bad words while he slipped back inside it again. When he had worked the last toe nail back through its proper hole, Jakamarra buttoned it up for him as carefully as ever, and you couldn't even see where the buttons were, so cleverly were they fitted.

Mole wriggled and squirmed around inside his skin shouting, 'No! No more! No more grit, no more grit!'

Then he said to Jakamarra, 'What were you saying before? Before we got so comfortable?'

'I said, will you please promise to leave Honey Ant alone!'

'Honey Ant? Honey Ant? I never go near Honey Ant. Sometimes Honey Ant builds his house where I happen to be digging, but that's his affair. He *will* build just where I'm going to dig!'

Jakamarra sighed. 'Well, will you promise not to dig up his house until he has given Wallaroo the club?'

'What club? Oh, all right, all right! Seeing you've been so helpful. Look, no grit,' he went on happily, wriggling and shifting around in joy.

'Goodbye then,' said Jakamarra and ran and ran back to Honey Ant with the news. Honey Ant gave the club to Wallaroo, and Wallaroo solemnly handed it to Jakamarra, who took it to Pelican, (when he could find him again among all his relatives). Old Pelican was delighted and pulled one of his longest,

softest feathers to give to Jakamarra. Bush Flies
travelled with Jakamarra all the way. Bush Flies
always do.

Jakamarra tucked the feather securely through his
hair-belt and ran and walked and trotted and skipped
and danced and frolicked back to the mountain
where Rain Spirit sat still as a stone. He took the
feather and began to tickle, ever so gently, under
Rain Spirit's chin. Rain Spirit began to gurgle and
shake with mirth but she kept her mouth firmly
closed. Jakamarra tickled a little harder. She opened
her eyes just a slit, two long, thin, golden, shining
slits. Her chin began to tremble while chuckles shook
her enormous body. Jakamarra stroked her again
with the feather and now she began to laugh.

The laughter rang and echoed round the high,
steep walls of the ranges and turned into thunder.
The golden eyes opened more and more, and from
them lightning flashed through the sky. At last her
lips parted and from them ran a stream of pure, clear
water. The sand darkened as it soaked up the wet,
and a small stream ran down the gully and out of
sight, downhill toward Bee's clump of straggly trees.

Jakamarra stopped tickling, the great mouth
stopped trickling water, and the sun dried the sand.
Rain Spirit closed her eyes and went back to sleep
to wait for the next Wet Time to arrive; for the old
men to waken her to loose the waters. In the pool
below Bee's trees, deep water sparkled and ran and
shimmered in the golden sunlight.

Jakamarra hid the feather carefully among the
stones in case he ever needed it again; then went to
Bee's nest. Bee gave him honey and he hurried with

it to Grandfather's camp. When he handed the sweet stuff to the old man, Grandfather unwrapped a small bundle and gave him some red ochre, enough to paint his body beautifully.

Jakamarra was delighted. He was just in time. His travelling had taken so long that it was the morning of the day of the full moon.

All day he ground and sifted the red ochre till it was fine as talc, ready for the painting. Late in the afternoon he was so weary from his travels that he thought he would rest a little. So he lay down in the cool dust and drifted off to sleep.

That night the full moon rose like a huge golden lantern in the eastern sky. All the people gathered round the fires that lit their dancing ground. Everybody sang, especially the song man, who accompanied himself by tapping two hard pieces of wood together. The women got up and danced and sang; then the men appeared from the darkness under the trees and they danced while the women sang and beat time with their hands. It was all very exciting and beautiful, and the party kept on until the moon shone from overhead. Everyone was waiting for Jakamarra, but to their surprise, he did not come.

Next morning Jakamarra woke when Bush Flies did. He yawned and stretched and scratched his head. Then with a shout he realized what had happened! He had been so tired from all his walking and running and skipping and leaping and travelling that he had slept all night and missed the dance altogether!

JUNGLE MOUSE

There was once a jungle mouse who lived deep in the wet rainforest with his brothers and sisters and parents and many relatives. This jungle mouse, whose name was Sak, was the smallest and ugliest of all the mice. He knew this to be true because when he was little and all his relatives had come to see the new children who were joining the Tribe of Jungle Mice, one said to his father, 'What are you going to call the little ugly one, the shrimp, the runt of the litter; the one whose eyes are too close together and whose nose is blunt and whose whiskers are too short?'

He heard his father reply, 'We will call him Sak.'

After his eyes had opened and he was growing bigger, he was playing with his brothers and sisters one day when he stopped playing and listened. Then he asked his mother, 'What is that faint and beautiful sound and where does it come from?' Because always in his mind, in the back of his head between his ears, he could hear music; gongs, drums, bells and a little flute.

His brothers and sisters laughed at him

because they couldn't hear anything, but his mother truly loved him, perhaps because he was the smallest and certainly he was the strangest of all her children. She listened hard, and when they were alone together one day she said, 'Little Sak, when I was a very small jungle mouse I used to think I could hear faint, beautiful music, but people said it was all imagination. When I grew to be a big mouse I stopped hearing it. Don't talk about it where your friends can hear or they will laugh at you.'

Sak took her advice and never mentioned it again, but when he was flitting from tree-bole to branch looking for ripe fruit that had fallen or been knocked from the high leafy canopy; and when he was hiding breathlessly silent in a terrified ball of fur from Tree Python who ate jungle mice he still seemed to hear the music.

One night when he was hidden in a crack in a tree-trunk waiting for darkness to come, the music seemed louder than ever before. He could hear the fruit bats swinging and eating fruit clumsily overhead and the scraps of fruit they were knocking and dropping were falling to the ground all ready for a jungle mouse's dinner. Then the sweet music called him. He peeked from his hollow and saw Toad squatting on the leaf-mould close by.

'Can you hear the music, Toad?' he asked excitedly.

Toad blinked round to see who was talking to him. 'Oh, it's you, Sak. Yes, I hear it sometimes. It belongs to Lord Tiger, Sak, and he is terrible. His skin is moonlight and darkness, and his mind is moonlight and darkness, too. Stay away from all that, Sak; or who knows what will happen to you.'

Many Kinds of Magic

'But it is so beautiful I want to hear it clearly.'

The warty old fellow looked hard at him. 'To hear that clearly and begin to know what it means you have to have Power, little Sak. Would you like to have Power? Because it is a difficult thing.'

'Oh yes, please, I'd like to have Power,' murmured Sak, still listening to the music.

'Then you will have to go to Bukit Raja the Mountain for that kind of Power,' said Toad. 'That's a long way to go through the swamps and the jungle. Better stay at home, little Sak, like all the other jungle mice.'

It was no use talking to Sak. He could not hear words any more. He could only hear the music calling to him. He did not even stay to gather the fruit that Fruit Bat had knocked down on the leafy floor. He trotted swiftly from shadow to shadow, skipping across the lighter spots and huddling, trembling with fear, every time he heard a scraping that might be Tree Python looking for him. Dawn lit the leaves high above him and the monkeys and parrots began their morning songs and he thought he had better find a hiding place for the day. His short legs were tired and his tail was sore from being dragged across the ground. He was very, very hungry.

Worst of all, he couldn't hear the music any more. Then he heard a voice calling to him. 'Hey! Hey, brother!' He looked for the owner of the voice, and there was another jungle mouse calling softly to him from a pile of fallen branches of a jungle palm. Swiftly Sak scuttled among the rustling leaves and thorny spines of the dead fronds. There he found the mouse, an old mouse, a big mouse with grey hair scattered through his mouse-brown coat and with sharp, button eyes.

'Who are you and where are you going?' asked the stranger.

'My name is Sak and I am going to Bukit Raja the Mountain to get some Power.'

'Huh! Thought you heard music, I suppose! Old Toad said you needed Power to hear it all the time, didn't he? He fooled me the same way when I was just a youngster like you.'

Sak felt uncomfortable, listening to the jeering words of this old mouse. He looked around. 'Oh, my,' he said. 'There's lots of seeds and fruit. What a lot of food you have here. There's great safety here under these spiky fronds, too. No one could find and eat a mouse under here! There's shelter from the monsoon rain and the floods wouldn't come here in the wet season either with their brown water. This is on a hill, isn't it?'

'That's right, young man. Now you listen to me. I thought I could hear music, and I talked to Toad and I started off to get Power. Then the music stopped and I found this place and I've lived here in great comfort ever since. But I have been very lonely with none of the Jungle Mouse Tribe to talk with and no one to inherit it from me after I die. Now you have come. I want you to stay and live with me, and when I die there will be someone to perform the death-rites for me. Then you would be master here and all this would be yours.'

Sak shook his head wonderingly. Suddenly the music and the dream it brought to him seemed very far away and unimportant. But he was wary, like all his people so he shook his head and said, 'Uncle, would you spare me a little food for I have run fasting all night? Would you spare me a corner of your shelter to sleep for I am weary? When I have eaten and slept I will tell you my thoughts.'

The old mouse agreed and Sak ate, then slept; rolled in a little soft brown ball of fur while the hours of daylight came and went.

While he slept, he dreamed. It seemed to him that he could hear the music once more. He followed it and came to a place of moonlight and shadows. The music was loud and clear and near. His heart swelled with joy and he was about to run forward to find the source of the beauty when, suddenly, there was the face of Lord Tiger only centimetres away! He could feel the heat of Tiger's breath and see his shining fangs! He screamed and woke to find the old mouse shaking his shoulder in a worried way. It was dusk.

'You were squeaking in a nightmare. I thought I'd better wake you in case a demon stole your body,' explained the old mouse.

'I was dreaming of Lord Tiger,' said Sak, his little ears flattened against the top of his head. 'He seems to be part of the music, somehow.'

'Well, nephew, you have slept and thought. Will you stay with me in this place of plenty?'

'I'm sorry, uncle, but the music calls me too strongly. I will go on to Bukit Raja the Mountain.'

The old mouse bowed his head and tears came from his round brown eyes. 'I should have gone! I should have gone!' he said.

Sak ate a little then ran on his way, scuttling

fearfully through the tangles and the clearings and the open places. He travelled all that night and by morning had reached some little hills. There he made a hasty breakfast from fruits and seeds and hid under a rotting fallen tree where he might be safe for the day. He was still frightened of Tree Python and terrified of Tiger. He woke at noon-day to the pitiful noise of someone weeping close by, someone crying sadly of a hopeless sorrow. Sak cautiously put his head out from his hiding place and saw Mrs Orang-utan, Mrs Old-Woman-Of-The-Forest, wailing softly on a branch close overhead. Sak was kindly, so he asked softly, 'Why are you so sad? Have you hurt yourself? Are you hungry? Has a demon been tormenting you?'

The ape had to peer and look very hard before she could see who was speaking to her. Then, blinking tears from her eyes, she said, 'No, it is none of these things. I have been to the oracle named She-Who-Sees-What-Will-Happen and she told me that I must die this day unless I get the tail of a jungle mouse to tie around my finger.

'This is a hard fate,' said Sak, edging back under the log and making sure his tail was well tucked in.

'Oh, I'm not crying for myself,' said Mrs Orang tearfully. 'It's my little one, my son. What will he do when his mother is dead and he cannot find food and there will be no one to care for him?'

'Doesn't he have any aunties?'

'They laugh at him and say he is small and ugly, a shrimp and a runt. They won't look after him.'

'Don't you listen to a word they say!' shrieked Sak indignantly. 'My relatives said that about me when

I was little and here I am, the bravest of them all, going where they would never dare to go and doing what they would never dare to do!'

Mrs Orang looked thoughtful. 'I'm sure my little boy would be a hero like you if only I didn't have to die,' she said. 'But I am cursed with this fate and now all is lost.' She began wailing and crying again and the tears rolled down her whiskers.

Now, his tail is the pride of every mouse. If a boy mouse wants to compliment a girl mouse he will tell her that her beauty is like the delicate tendril of a jungle creeper, and a girl mouse will say his courage is strong and sturdy as a twig of fern. Sak thought very hard about what he should do next. The ape was growing dimmer of eye as he watched, and becoming weaker; and her little son was nuzzling vainly at her and crying shrilly while she hugged him and tried to comfort him. Sak could bear it no longer.

'Mother, Mother, do you have sharp teeth?' he cried.

Mrs Orang nodded feebly.

'Then bite off my tail, quickly, quickly; for I am a jungle mouse and your salvation,' he said before he could think again and change his mind. He slipped from his hiding-place and the ape snapped once with her sharp yellow teeth. Then Sak felt a tearing pain and a continuing ache so he cried aloud, but his cries were drowned by the shout of joy from Mrs Orang. She hastily tied the tail around her finger and immediately was well again.

She rose from where she clung to the branch and bowed before him three times with her palms pressed together in front of her, and she made her son bow also.

'You have saved my life and my son's life and I will help you if I can,' she said humbly.

Sak was so surprised he almost forgot his pain. 'Please get up, Mother Orang, before someone comes along and thinks I might be someone important,' he said uncomfortably. 'I am only jungle mouse, very weak and afraid and frightened; foolish enough to follow music no one else can hear. It's a long journey, my legs are tired and I am hurting badly, but I am glad you are well and there is no doubt that your son will grow to be a King among the Old-Men-Of-The-Forest for he is strong and princely.'

'Where is your music calling you?' asked Mrs Orang.

'I am going to Bukit Raja the Mountain to try to get Power,' said Sak, 'but I am not sure if I will get there or if there will be Power there for me if I do; or even if I would be worthy to receive Power if it is indeed there.'

'You have helped me, and I will help you,' said Mrs Orang. 'I will make a little basket from palm fronds and line it with soft moss and hang it from my shoulders. You can lie in it like a baby in a cradle and I will take you to the foot of Bukit Raja the Mountain for I know where it is. I was born near the foot of it, though I have never dared walk or climb there, for the mountain belongs to Lord Tiger, and the peak is always covered in clouds.'

She stripped palm fronds with her clever fingers and made a mouse-sized basket. She part filled it with soft moss and put Sak gently into it. His tail had stopped bleeding by now, but he was sick at heart for it hurts to lose your beauty. Mrs Orang hung the basket from her shoulder, and her son gripped her very firmly. Then she leapt through the tree-tops at great speed, swinging and running along branches, hanging from jungle vines, leaping from tree to tree. Sak swung and swung like a sailor in a hammock and at last he slept. When he woke it was almost dark, his wound felt much better and Mrs Orang had halted in a huge durian tree. She was feeding on the delicious smelly fruit and her son was feeding also.

'Wake up, wake up little Lord,' she said gently between bites. 'We are at the foot of Bukit Raja the Mountain and it is nearly time for me to sleep. Where will you spend the night?'

'Take me to the bottom of the tree, beautiful mother,' said Sak feebly. 'I will eat and then I will climb the mountain and see what might befall me. I think I hear the music again though it is very faint.'

She ran down the vertical trunk and the lacing of vines as though it was a broad ladder and placed him gently in a hollow where he just fitted snugly. She gave him the best and ripest durian fruit she had saved for him, enough for three meals for a jungle mouse. She placed the palms of her hands flat together in front of her face and bowed her head three times then sprang away up to find a nest high in the topmost branches where she would be safe for the night. Mouse ate some of the fruit, then began his journey uphill in the dark.

At first he found it hard to keep his balance as he ran without his tail to help, but gradually he grew more accustomed to this. He was sure he could hear the music again now, though it was just a breath of melody on the edge of silence. He climbed stealthily uphill all night, thinking all the time that his journey couldn't last much longer. Twice he heard Lord Tiger coughing; the first time far off, the second time much closer. He trembled and hurried on each time, climbing steadily. When daylight came he was at the top of a slope and thought he might have reached his goal, but when the warm mist cleared from the tree-tops, he found he had only reached the top of one of the foothills and that Bukit Raja the Mountain loomed before him; high, high, high; so high the clouds hid the stony peak. Jungle Mouse sighed and found a crevice in a stone where he could sleep safely. He ate some little berries from a vine, and curled up in the crevice. At first he couldn't get to sleep without his tail to wrap around the end of his nose but he was so weary that at last he slept.

It was noon when Sak wakened, trembling nervously. He thought at first it was the rumbling of a thunderstorm that had wakened him, then he peered out and found to his horror Lord Tiger was lying on the rock where he was tucked into the crevice, purring gently. It was this rumbling that had wakened him! Sak was terrified. Everyone knew Lord Tiger was King, that he had great Power, that he ruled everywhere, that his word was Law! This Tiger who was watching him was a very old Tiger Lord but he was still full of strength and wisdom and he didn't seem angry. Also, the music was louder than mouse had ever heard before, so loud and lovely that it almost reassured him.

Tiger-lord finished polishing his face with his huge

paws and looked at Sak.

'Ahey, little brother,' he said. 'What are you doing so close to Bukit Raja and so far from your own country?'

'Great Lord!' said Sak, holding his tiny paws together in front of his pointed nose and bowing low three times. 'I have heard music and it called me. I have travelled with the help of friends to this place where perhaps I may hear it more clearly.'

'You must have also found trouble, for that which was your pride is no longer with you,' said Tiger delicately and politely. He meant the mouse's tail, of course, but it is the duty of a King not to embarrass his subjects unless he must do so to show justice.

'Lord, it is nothing,' said Sak, ashamed.

'Come out and show me!' ordered Lord Tiger.

It was the hardest thing Sak had ever done. Every nerve in his little soft body seemed to be on fire with fear, but his heart was brave and the music sounded louder as he crept humbly from the hole and knelt before his lord.

Tiger looked hard at him. 'This was bitten off!' he rumbled and his eyes were red and fierce. 'Who dared hurt you?'

'Great striped Lord, it was my gift to that person.'

The fire died from Tiger's eyes and he looked rather sadly at Mouse.

'So! A gift should be freely given and freely taken. There is no blame, then. But I have come to ask for a gift, too,' said Tiger.

Mouse said nothing, but his heart sank in despair.

'I do not command you in this, little one, but I am the Guardian of the Mountain and those who pass must give me a gift,' said Tiger.

'Take what you will, master,' said Sak.

'Freely offered, I said. Well, I will give you a choice. One of two things you must leave with me, Mouse. Either your hearing or your sight. Before you pass me you must become either blind or deaf! Which do you choose?'

Sak lay flat on the ground for he had not thought the choice would be so terrible. He could not even feel the rough stone under him, so numb with misery was he. It was a dreadful choice.

'What would happen if I did not want to pass, and went back down the mountain?' he asked, and he was so upset that he forgot to call Tiger by his proper titles and dignities.

'Nothing will happen to you. You will remain as you are for the rest of your life. You may even live very happily, who knows?'

'Does the music come from the mountain?' asked Sak.

'It is there,' said Tiger.

'Then take my eyes, Lord, for I wish to hear the music,' said Sak humbly.

'If I take your sight how will you climb? How will you see to go up? How will you escape Tree Python if he should come?'

'Lord, the music means more to me, and if I can hear it then I can follow it.'

'You came here seeking Power. What use is Power to a blind mouse?'

'I do not want Power any more, only the music.'

'You have chosen!' said Lord Tiger, and the sun went out for Sak.

Next moment he knew he was alone, the King was gone. Yet Sak did not feel lonely for now the music swelled in his head until he was dizzy with joy. He knew the way to go to reach it, too. 'Night and day are all one to me now,' thought Sak, and he did not wait for the cooler wind of night and darkness. He began to climb up the hot rocks. He stumbled over roots and stones. Several times through the lifting sound of the music he thought he heard the sound of Tree Python's scaly belly rasping on the rocks toward him but his head was full of the joy of music and his heart was brave as only the heart can be that has looked eye to eye with Lord Tiger. Sak did not stop for food or sleep, he grimly found the upward slope and went forward. After a long time he came to a level place and sank to the ground. The music in his head turned to voices, many, many voices; singing the tunes mice most love.

'We are the Brotherhood of the World!' sang the voices. 'We are no-legs and two-legs and four-legs and many-legs. We are wings and fins; blind white ants and far-seeing eagles, honey-bees and beetles and little dancing flies. We are elephant in the forest and otter among the seaweeds. We are the eyeless shells in the shallow water and luminous squid of the black deeps, we are the sardine shoal on the surface and the gulls that feed upon them and the eagles that rob the gulls. We are Toad and Old-Woman-Of-The-Forest and we are Tree Python too. Now we are you. You are one of us and we are all of you, for we are the Brotherhood of all the World and you have joined us.'

Mouse wept for joy at the beauty of the singing. He felt what seemed to be a great wind blow through him and suddenly he changed. He saw again; light and trees and clouds, rocks and sky and the deep blue sea of air hanging over his head. He saw the wind coiling around him and caressing the tree-tops far below him, and he was on top of Bukit Raja the Mountain.

'I am glad,' he said aloud. 'I have heard the music. I have heard the voices. What mouse has ever been so blessed before?'

Then the Voice whispered in his ears, louder than the music, the gentle music he would never lose again, 'You are not Mouse any more. Now you are Tiger!'

And he was.

EVAN THE MUSCLES

Away up the top end of a valley in the mountains of Wales, where it was only a crack in the rock lived a widow woman who had a son named Evan ap Thomas. She was a clever little soul, wrinkled as a Christmas apple and so short in stature that her sharp black hat looked as tall as she did herself. Evan, though only a lad of eighteen summers, was a thickset boy. He had a body round and hard as an oak-tree trunk and a head like a cannon-ball, all circular and with very little brains in it.

From babyhood he had been a powerful thing. When he cried, the stones cracked and chipped in the walls of the cottage and bits of the thatch wisped off; when he kicked with his legs he pushed the end out of the cradle. He grew up so sturdy his friends and the few neighbours called him Evan the Muscles because of his great strength. He was mostly a placid child, and good-natured; smiling at his food when it was put in front of him and eating it faster than a fire eats stubble. A great one for his platter, was Evan, though a worry to his mother to keep it filled and on the table before him. With nourishment from goat's milk and cheese, mountain mutton, wheaten bread and small beer he grew and grew fast, not so much upward as sideways and through from front to back so he looked much in shape as a great, sturdy barrel. He got no schooling save what his mother could spare, and that was little enough; but he could write his name like a christian and count his money. What more than that would such a sturdy lad need to make his way in the world?

It came to the widow one day while she was watching him hold the cow above his head and shake it around that it was time he went out into the world to earn his own bread and perhaps a loaf or two over for his poor little mother. But she was curious, so before she sent him on his way she asked, 'Evan bach, why are you holding up the cow and shaking it?'

'I had a thought to save you trouble, mam,' said the lad. 'I was watching you winding and winding at that old churn this morning to make the butter separate from the milk, and I thought that if it was done before you milked the cow what a lot of trouble you might be saved.'

Then his mother was sure it was time that he went off to seek his fortune whatever, but all she said was, 'Come here, but first put the cow down gently. There, that's neat for you.' Then she trotted away to the cottage calling for him to follow. He bounded down the slope like a goat, shaking the boulders and astonishing the rabbits to where she stood by the cottage door. 'Wait you here,' said she, and vanished inside.

Evan waited, and after a time she came out with

a bundle and other things. 'It's time you went out and found work for yourself fit for you to do,' said she.

'All right, mam, but where will I go and what will I do?'

'Go on downhill till you find a town where they hire men to work in the fields and byres and at the shepherding, and hire yourself out for money and keep for a year. When you have made your fortune, bring it home to me. Don't let me see you till then, for I'm worn out finding food for the both of us.'

'I'll do that, mam,' said the lad. 'What's in the bundle and what's these other things?'

'In the bundle are two loaves, a cheese and the last three pennies of our wealth. That should nourish you until tomorrow, anyway.'

'What's these other things?' asked the young man, picking them up and shaking them.

'That's an old iron shirt that was your grand-father's, it should wear well. The others are a pair of iron boots for you.'

'What's boots?' asked Evan, for he had never seen such things in his life.

'Those are things you put on your feet so you don't go bumping your toes on the old rocks. Mostly they're made from leather, but those are of iron, and they served your grandfather all his life, so maybe they'll do for you as well.'

Evan was so proud to have such fine things that nothing would do but that he put them on straight away. He slipped the iron shirt on over his head, though it fitted a bit snug, then he put on the iron boots after his mam had showed him about which was the left one and which was the right and how to tell the difference. Then he picked up his mam and kissed her goodbye so she had trouble speaking for a week afterwards; took up his bread and cheese, tied the three pennies in a knot in the corner of his iron shirt so he wouldn't lose them, and strode off down the valley. As he went his mam could hear the clanging of his boots on the rocks like the sound of the bells of Rhymney, but louder and not so musical.

The valley grew deeper and deeper and wider and wider as Evan walked, till in a while he was clanging along a broad road beside a wide river and the mountains had shrunk to a pile of blue in the sky far behind him. He grew a little hungry so he sat on a felled tree-trunk beside the road and unwrapped the bundle his mam had given him. As he took out the food, three men stepped from behind the hedge where they had been hiding. Rough fellows, they were, carrying swords and shields and long, black Welsh bows, and with quivers full of arrows slung across their shoulders.

'Good day to you!' said Evan cheerfully, for his mam had taught him to be polite.

'Now, boyo, just hand over your food and money and you'll come to little harm,' said the biggest and blackest looking of the ruffians.

'That's no way to talk to an honest country boy who hasn't eaten anything for hours,' said Evan calmly. 'You're welcome to a bite if you say "please" and be polite, otherwise you can look elsewhere for feeding.'

For all his politeness they took arrows from their quivers and shot them at him with their bows. The

Many Kinds of Magic

arrows rang and crumpled when they hit his iron coat and made him notice what they were doing. 'That was unfriendly of you,' said he and he got to his feet carefully, putting his food aside, for he had once stepped in his dinner and didn't like it much afterwards so didn't want to do the same again. The men drew their swords and ran towards him. Evan picked up the first to reach him and swung him by the ankles like a club, knocking the others down. This did no good to the one he was using, so soon he had all three lying side by side on the grass.

He tried out their bows to see if one or other might suit him, but they all broke when he pulled them. He skimmed their shields away like plates into a lake nearby, then he tried the swords but they bent and crumpled when he tested them so he tied them into knots and laid them by. He sat down again on the stump and went on with his dinner, watching the three figures beginning to stir as their senses came back to them.

Just as his mouth was full of wheatcake and cheese a troop of the King's horsemen came galloping round the curve of the road and up to where he sat. They couldn't see the robbers because of the hedgerow but they halted when they saw Evan.

'What are you doing, boy?' roared their Captain.

'I'm eating my dinner, though just how soon I'll get done with all these interruptions I can't say,' said Evan when his mouth was empty enough to speak.

'You be careful, young man, for the Three Black Brothers of Aberystwith are around hereabouts, robbing and swearing and murdering and we're hunting them!' said the officer.

Evan chewed for a bit, for thinking didn't come easily to him, then he said, 'Would they be three ugly black men with bows and arrows and swords and bucklers and no sort of politeness about them?'

'That's the villains!' said the officer.

'Oh, you'll find them lying behind the hedgerow over there among the stones, looking so peaceful. I put them there a while ago.'

The Captain and his men leapt from their fine horses and ran round the hedge. They fell on the robbers with glad shouts and bound them with iron chains. The robbers were waking by now and began to curse and swear and struggle, but when the King's horsemen dragged them to where they could again see Evan they changed their song and begged the officer to tuck them safe away in a dungeon where the lad couldn't come at them any more.

'For,' said the ugliest brother, 'it's an unfair thing that a man like that should be let out on the roads upsetting honest thieves and tying their swords in knots and letting everyone think they were only a simple bumpkin and easy prey.' Then the horsemen went away with the thieves running beside their stirrups.

Evan ate the last of the food and washed it down with a gallon or two of water from the river, then hurried on. By the time it was darkening with the dusk he was feeling hungry again, his wishbone flapping in his empty inwards, when he saw a town in the distance. By running as fast as he could (and making a noise like a blacksmith beating on an anvil with his boots), he got to the gates just as the men-at-arms were closing them for the night. He hastily

Many Kinds of Magic

slipped through and suddenly found himself in the narrowest place he had ever been in his life.

It was only a street with buildings on both sides but the lad had never before seen a house that didn't stand all alone by itself. He walked through the dimness between the overhanging walls and came at last to the market-place where a lot of people were listening to a man who stood on the tail of a cart and spoke to them with great passion.

'What are we to do?' the man was shouting. 'Tomorrow is the hiring fair, and *he'll* be coming down from the hill and *he* won't let any of us get on with our hiring until *he* is suited with a servant for the next year. Oh, *he* offers good wages, but who ever lived to collect them? Nobody will go to work for such a one, and they will not offer and *he* won't let us start our hiring until *he* has got his man. The King ought to send an army to root *him* out, *him* and that dragon of his.'

'What is the trouble?' asked Evan of a man standing listening.

'It's the two-headed ogre from up above,' said the man, jerking his head to indicate the mountain overlooking the town and its rim still showing a tinge of light from the sunset. 'He's twelve feet high, or maybe 3.6576 metres, if you come from Gaul, and his two heads are mostly arguing with one another if one of them isn't asleep. Every year he comes to the hiring fair to find a manservant to hew his firewood and carry in his water, but he always loses his temper with his men before the year is up and if you are working for an ogre with two heads (even though one sleeps most of the time), that has a red dragon for a watchdog, that can be fatal for you, boy!'

'It seems to me the folks around here are too easy on such a one as that,' said Evan. 'It's time he was taught respect.'

'If you're so brave you might like to hire yourself out to him in the morning, and so let the rest of us get on with our hiring in peace,' said the man, looking disagreeable. 'It's easy to see you're fresh from the hills yourself and a bit simple with it I shouldn't be surprised, so I'll say no more.'

He walked away, leaving Evan to look round at the stalls lining the market. There was one that drew him by the nose. Outside was a notice reading:

ALL YOU CAN EAT FOR A PENNY

Now, Evan couldn't read, but he could smell the pot of oatmeal and the mutton stew with onions bubbling in the two great cauldrons, so he paused outside the booth. The cook winked at the cloth merchant who had the next stall and said to Evan, 'All you can eat for two pennies, boyo!' for he could see Evan was fresh from the mountains and maybe couldn't read his letters.

Evan thought this was the finest offer anyone had ever made him.

'I'll accept that offer, friend, though I should warn you I'm sharp-set and have a great hunger travelling with me.'

'You've come to the right place, then,' said the cook, winking again at his neighbour.

Evan sat at the rough table and said, 'Bring on the food.'

Many Kinds of Magic

'First, the money,' said the cook. The lad untied the corner of his knotted shirt and took two of his mam's pennies out.

'Here you are with my goodwill. Now lead on with the victuals and I'll cry halt when I've come to the end of my appetite!'

After the first half hour of his eating, word went round among the folk in the market-place that a miracle was taking place at the stall of the cook. People gathered in a respectful circle and watched while Evan ate and ate. The cauldron of stew was showing its bottom through the gravy and the oatmeal in the other pot was ebbing like the tide at Anglesey. The stall-holder was almost in tears by this and begging Evan to show mercy, but the cloth merchant had told of his cheating ways and the people cheered Evan on. A fat farmer went and bought the lad a small keg of ale to help his eating, and he ate and drank steadily until all was gone and the stall-holder was in tears.

'Thank you, friend,' said Evan, letting his belt out two notches and rising at last when he was sure the keg was empty and sides of the pots were polished clean. 'When I go back to the mountains I will tell all my friends about the generous man at the hiring fair and I tell all you good people hereabouts this is the finest and cheapest cook I have met who ever stirred stew in pot.'

The man groaned and wouldn't be comforted at all, only he begged Evan never to tell any of his friends about it in case they might have appetites like his own. Evan rose and went on to find a place where he might stretch out for the night.

Now there was a man in that town named Black Davy who made his living by offering travellers a bed and then daggering them to death while they slept, for the sake of their clothes and their little bit of money. He would cast their bodies from a window of his house into the river that flowed wide, deep and fast by the walls of the town. He chose only strangers so no one would miss them and ask questions about their disappearance. When he saw Evan walking slowly along, looking up at the buildings in wonder, he hailed him.

'Are you seeking a warm bed for the night?' asked Black Davy. 'In my loft is fine hay with no old thistles in it, it's the same as if you wrapped yourself in a wool blanket, the heat that's in it.'

'What's your fee?' asked Evan.

'I'll give you your bed and breakfast for a penny,' said Black Davy, cunning as the fox of Abergavenny.

'It's a bargain, then,' said Evan, and turned into the doorway.

He was thinking to himself that travelling was a fine thing. There were kind souls all through the world so he could hardly believe it. Here he had had the finest dinner a man could wish for, and now he was to sleep warm under a roof away from the stars and the wind and the rain.

Black Davy showed him to the pile of hay and left him to sleep. Evan took off his iron boots and thoughtfully turned them inside out, for they had been rubbing his unaccustomed feet and he hoped to make them more supple. He turned them back to shape again, stroking them with his thumbs, then put them neatly side by side beside the pile of hay, knelt, and said his prayers and soon was sleeping so deep and snoring so loud the pigs complained six houses off.

In the dark of middle night when the cocks wake and turn on their perches and crow once, a dim figure slipped silently into the room where a great hump under the hay showed where Evan was asleep. The figure carried a long, sharp dagger. It was Black Davy. He crept silently toward the horrid noise of snoring, but all at once he tripped over the iron boots in the dark, hurting all ten of his toes and the littlest ones most of all.

Evan was dreaming he was home asleep in his mam's byre where he slept always with the cow and when he heard the clank he thought it was his mam coming to do the early milking, the way she would be rattling the pail.

'Don't you be fussed coming in, mam,' he called. 'I'll send the cow out to you through the window!' Still sleeping soundly he reached out and took Black Davy by the ankles and tossed him easily out the window where he had put so many dead travellers. Davy fell twenty metres and landed in a stony place, where he broke his neck before bouncing on into the river and floating away; and that was good enough for him, too.

Evan slept on in the hay and it was hunger gnawing and biting inside him like a ferret that woke him at last. It was broad day-light. He got up and went out to the kitchen place, calling to his landlord for his breakfast, but no one came. He looked around, and there was a side of bacon and twelve brown eggs beside the fire, and a griddle to cook them with. It wasn't long before the lad had sliced the bacon and sizzled it, and fried the eggs. These, with a quartern loaf and a pail of milk made a fine breakfast for him. He cried out once again for his landlord, but still no one came, which was not surprising because Davy was ten kilometres off downstream by this and making a fine dinner for the eels and the fishes. So Evan left the penny on the table among the dirty dishes, he being honest, and went out to greet the morning and meet the day.

The hiring ground was like a fox among the geese for turmoil when he got there. People ran hither and thither. Staring over the stone wall of the town and into the market-place were two of the ugliest faces he had ever seen.

'Who is it to be, then?' roared one of the heads looking in, while the other slept soundly. 'Who'll serve me for a year and a day? I'll feed him full and pay him five silver coins for his year's hire. Who will it be?'

The old, white-haired Mayor came out of the throng, pushed from behind by the aldermen.

'You'll get no one from this place to work for you,' said the Mayor when the others had told him what to say. 'What happened to Big Pugh the Plough, what happened to Dai Blacksmith? They engaged to work for you and no one has seen them since then. Who dares to work for such a master? Go your ways, Thug the Ogre, you'll get no bondman here.'

The ogre roared with rage. 'I'll get no servant, you say? If I get no servant I'll let my red dragon off his chain and send him to visit you and what'll happen to your daughters then? Saint George is dead,

Lancelot is dead and so is the Heir of Lambton. Where are the heroes these times? Besides, there would be meself to deal with as well. Now, who'll be my servant? Five pieces of silver and a full belly, morning, noon and night for a year's work!'

Evan said to the man who stood beside him, 'How many pennies would go to make a piece of silver, for to tell the truth I've never seen a piece of silver.'

'For a piece of silver you would get a hundred pennies,' said the man.

'That's for me, then,' said Evan. He clanked his way to the middle of the square and stood beside the Mayor and the aldermen.

'Hey, Thug the Ogre, what kind of vittles and ale do you serve? If they're enough to fill a stout fellow like me then I'm your man, but I want nothing of small beer and mouldy bread and bacon, if that's what you offer.'

Thug seemed a little upset by these words but he soon rallied. 'You'll have no complaint of the eating and drinking if you come. My brewing is of the best, and as for the boiling and broiling, baking and roasting and grilling I've had no grumbles. It's all of the best. Will you engage to cut my wood and haul my water for a year and a day for five silver pieces?'

'Aye, I'll do those things, and clasp hands with you in front of His Holiness the Mayor on the bargain,' said Evan, shaking aside the Mayor and three aldermen who were trying to stop him.

Thug shouted with pleasure and leaned over the wall with his great hand like a side of leather to grip hands with Evan. Evan seized him and shook with such goodwill that the ogre moved up and down and stones fell from the wall. The ogre's other head, which had slept through all the roaring and shouting, opened its eyes and asked 'Brother, what was that?'

'I've hired us a man for the year,' said the first head.

The sleepy one said, 'What man is that?'

'That one there!' and the great hand pointed at Evan.

The sleepyhead looked at Evan with his iron boots and his iron shirt and said, 'I think you might have made a bad bargain, but I'll leave all that to you.' Then it shut its eyes and went back to sleep.

Thug looked at Evan doubtfully for a minute, then he laughed and said, 'Come along, little man. We'll be off home now.'

'With all my heart,' cried Evan. He leaped over the wall and followed the ogre up the mountain to the cave where he lived.

There was a great cavern in the rocks, and chained at one side of the opening was a dragon. Not a huge dragon such as used to trouble the world one time but a nasty-looking small dragon as tall as Evan. It lay in the sun with a little puff of smoke curling up from its nose like a badly swept chimney. Its breath smelt dreadful, like smouldering sulphur and burning wool. It snarled at the ogre, but when it saw Evan it sprang into the air as though to attack him, and he could see it was held by a huge bronze chain welded to a ring set in its nose like the one worn by the Bull of Derry Macbrandy in the far-off land of the Picts.

'Hold on now!' said Thug to the dragon. 'This is me new man, Evan. If you go scorching him he'll never be fit to chop and carry. Leave him alone, you hear?'

The dragon lay down again and seemed to sleep, but Evan could see it was watching him through a crack in its eyelids where its golden eyeball shone like a candle through a chink in a board.

Even asked the ogre, 'Where do I eat and where do I sleep, and what would you have me do to begin my work?'

'In the back of the cavern there's a place where you can make a bed. Down the valley below is a stream where you'll get water, and here's the bucket to fetch it up. On top of the mountain is the forest where you'll get the wood, and by the hearth is the place to chop it and stack it. The axe is just inside the door, if you can lift it. We'll see about the food when you've begun to earn it.' Saying which, the ogre strode off down the valley.

So Evan took a waterbutt down to the stream and filled it rather than carry a bucket back and forth; though the cask held enough for an ogre to drink for a week.

'Me head is saving me legs,' said Evan. He did this with all the huge water-butts and stood them neat in a row along the back of the cave. By now it was lunchtime, but no sign of the ogre appeared, so he went on working. He ran up to the top of the mountain and pulled over two great oak trees. He snapped the limbs from them and carried one under each arm down the hill to where the dragon slept.

The dragon looked at him and sneered.

'The others always cut the wood upalong and

brought it down a piece at a time,' remarked the dragon.

Evan was enchanted, and dropped the logs. 'What, such a pretty dragon, and you can talk as well! You're the wonder of the world, you are! You fume so hearty and glow so bright and talk like a preacher as well! I can see us having wonderful times, you and me; times we'll sit and tell each other stories about the things we've seen and done!'

The dragon stopped looking fierce and a puff of steam came from the corners of its eyes. It was weeping.

'I've seen nothing but this place, and done nothing but scuffle and erupt at the end of this chain!' he said. 'That one inside there named Thug found me just after I came from the egg. Pretty words he gave me, said he'd put a ring in me nose would make me the envy of every one of my kind I'd meet. Then the cruel thing chained me here for a watch-dragon, and little have I seen or done since then.'

'Wasn't that the cruel thing to do,' exclaimed Evan.

'I've never even seen a princess to talk to, and that's what dragons enjoy most,' said the unfortunate creature, and jets of steam sprang from its eyes like the safety valve on Cosher Bailey's engine.

'I haven't seen one meself, though I've looked round the world more than you,' said Evan. 'But there, they can't be so plentiful you know, these days. Not like the old times when as like as not you'd find them sitting round everywhere, weeping and waiting to be rescued from cruel knights or giants and dr . . .,' and his voice trailed away uncertainly.

'Go on! Say it! Dragons!' said the little dragon sadly.

'Well, forget it. We aren't likely to be seeing any princesses up here, are we,' said Evan hastily.

'Shows all you know!' said the dragon bitterly. 'He's got one in that little cave over there. He goes and talks to her every night but won't let her out for a breath of fresh air or a word or two with a kindly young dragon.'

'Why does he keep her?' asked Evan, amazed.

'I don't know,' said the dragon. 'Same reason other ogres do, I suppose. They just seem to collect princesses.'

'Never you mind, boy,' said Evan, patting the dragon gently on top of its head so its chin bounced up and down on the ground. 'I'm here now and I'll talk to you whenever I get a minute.'

'That's kind of you. But I'm not a boy, I'm a girl dragon. Ah, don't apologize, it makes no difference unless you're another dragon. I'll be glad of the conversation, mind you. Thug's other head is all right when it can stay awake; it's friendly enough, but he's a cruel one.'

Just then Thug returned and went into the cavern, shouting, 'I'm not paying you good silver to stand there and gossip like a hen-wife! Get along with your work!'

So Evan did.

When he hit the oak-trunks they split every time, and when he carried the billets in he did so by the cartload. By the time the sun was westering the wood-place was piled high with enough fuel for two hard winters and all the waterbutts along the back of the cave were overflowing. Evan sat on the empty bucket beside the hearth with the axe across his knees and waited for his tea, for he was sharp-set with hunger from missing his lunch. His breakfast seemed a long way back, to him.

Thug came in and looked around in surprise at the work he had done. 'Well! usually it takes them months to get all that done, but the sooner it's over the sooner to sleep, I suppose,' he said.

'I'll not sleep till I've had me dinner,' said Evan stubbornly.

'Ah, but you mightn't be needing it, after all,' said Thug, sliding his hand along to the long, sharp knife he wore in his belt.

'Oh, but I will, then,' said Evan drowsily, lounging back on his bucket. 'A double lot, too, for I missed me lunch.'

'Here it is for you, then,' said Thug, lunging at him with the knife.

Evan threw up his arms in surprise and lost his balance. He fell backward off the bucket and landed in the hot coals near the fire. Trying to get up in a hurry, he forgot the axe he was still holding in his hand, and it swung in a great arc and, unluckily for Thug, the edge of the axe met with his throat just about where the knob of his Adam's apple stuck out like a knot in a branch. The sleepyhead woke up with cries of 'Where are we? What's happening?' as its ugly twin was chopped from the neck next door and shot out the door of the cave to be lost in the dark that was beginning to fall.

Evan felt terribly guilty about what he had done, but the sleepyhead was wide awake by now. It hastily ran the ogre's body across to a chest standing near the back wall and brought out a jar of magic ointment, with which it daubed the wounded neck. The wound healed straight away, but there was no chance of Thug's head ever being joined on again, and now the other head was wide awake and looking round, trying to discover what had happened. When it saw Evan rolling in the cinders, trying to get the axe out of the way, it said, 'That's quite enough! Don't you think you've done enough damage?'

'Oh, I am sorry, I do apologize!' said Evan. 'I don't suppose there's any way we might stick you back together? It was an accident of course, I never meant to harm anyone.'

'What's done is done and there's no point in crying over spilt milk, though it was careless of you,' said the sleepyhead. 'Anyway, him that's gone was very selfish. He'd never let me go off studying Latin and Greek and geography and natural history like I wanted to. Do you know, he would hit me so often for wanting to be a scholar that in the end I just went to sleep all the time and let him have everything his way. Now I'm going to do what I want to do, and he won't be around to stop me any more, or be sarcastic, or hit me when I'm not looking.'

'Well, for now, let's have some food, for you do get hungry talking and I haven't had me dinner,' said the lad.

'Now, that's a good idea,' said the sleepyhead, who seemed to have a much nicer nature than his departed brother. 'I'm peckish myself. The food's in that big cupboard, I think.'

The two of them roasted an ox and cooked a bag of oatmeal and ate hearty till they could eat no more. They loosened their straining belts and were drinking buckets of ale when there came a whimpering sound from outside. Evan sprang to his feet.

'There's cruel I am, forgetting the poor dragon,' said he. 'And her without even a little princess to eat.'

'I knew there was something I was going to do but the skill and wonder of your conversation drove it from my mind,' said the ogre. 'I think we should let the poor beast go free.'

'I'll do it, I'm the servant here,' said Evan. He went to the cave mouth and called the dragon. 'I'll just take this away from you, girl,' he said. 'Don't breathe fire for just a minute or you'll scorch my fingers. There, that's took that old ring away. You're a free woman from here on out.'

'Do you mean I can fly away?'

'Anywhere you like.'

'I'll go round the wide world to eastern parts, then,' said the dragon. 'There's not so many of us dragons left in Wales, but I heard I have many relatives and kin among the watery clouds far off. Sit on pearly thrones, they do, and spout water on the land below. Yes, that will be a change from this dreary cave. You're a good man, Evan bach. I'll never forget you.'

The dragon unfolded what had seemed to be two horny ridges on her back and Evan saw the filmy grace and delicate shimmering colours of her wings spread before him. She launched herself into the air and he watched as she dwindled into a tiny pinpoint of light among the stars until she was gone.

He went back into the cave and found the ogre still sipping ale. 'The dragon's gone to China,' he said.

The ogre didn't seem to hear him.

'Appleby? Batchelor? Christmas? Dangerfield?

Eddington? Fletcher? . . . Yes, Fletcher!' said the ogre with great satisfaction.

'Fletcher?'

'My new name. One can hardly be expected to pursue one's studies of etiquette and the finer things in life if one is named Thug. I will call myself Fletcher!'

'It's a good enough name for an arrow-maker, so it ought to serve well enough for a scholar,' said Evan. 'You know, Fletcher, I keep feeling that there is something else I should be remembering.'

'The Reverend Doctor Fletcher, D.D., Ph.D., maybe,' went on the ogre dreamily.

'I know what it is!' said Evan. 'The princess.'

'What princess?'

'Your brother has a princess hidden away in the little cave over there.'

'Good heavens, we must free her,' said Fletcher, rising.

'Maybe it should be me that does that; she mightn't be ready to accept you yet,' said the young man. 'I'll tell you what. I'll just slip across and do that while you hunt for your brother's treasure-chest, for he owes me some money for the work I did for him.'

'I'll find where he kept the money, then, while you free the princess.'

Evan went out the door again. For a few long minutes he stood staring at the sky where he had last seen the dragon, because it had been a most beautiful thing to see. He sighed at last, and clanked across to the door at the mouth of the little cave.

'Princess? Hey, Princess, are you there? Can you hear me?'

'It's no good you trying your old blandishments on

me, I'm a good princess,' said a voice on the other side of the door.

'I'm not trying them – things, what you said. Me name's Evan the Muscles and I've come to rescue you.'

'Are you a prince?'

'Well, no, I'm not,' said Evan humbly. 'I've mostly followed what me friend Fletcher calls agricultural and herding employment.'

'Then I'll just wait till a prince comes along to free me from the evil ogre Thug. My father the King has promised half his kingdom and my hand in marriage to the prince that kills the ogre and sets me free.'

Evan cleared his throat in an embarrassed way because it now seemed to his slow understanding that he might have messed things up for the Princess's plans.

At last he said, 'Well, I'm sorry, but Thug has gone the good Lord knows where, and the dragon's flown off to China and there's no one here but me and Fletcher; and he tells me he's off to a place called Oxenford to learn to be a proper scholard, and I'm going home to me mam as soon's I get me money.'

There was silence for a while, then the door opened a crack and then wide, and out came the Princess. She was a lot taller than Evan and she was very thin and her hair hung down loose over her face the way you couldn't see it at all except that her nose thrust through the falling locks like the prow of a Viking long-ship.

She had a hard look at Evan through her hair and down her nose and said, 'Are you sure Thug has gone away?'

'In a manner of speaking he has and he hasn't. I'm afraid there's been a bit of an accident, your Worship. He fell over me feet and I cut off his head when I wasn't looking though I meant him no harm, clumsy ogre that he was though probably good-hearted in spite of all his rough ways.'

The Princess shook her hair back from her face and she was not a beautiful princess but a narrow-cheeked one with a sour face as if she had drunk the vinegar by mistake.

'You're very ugly,' she said frowning.

'Well, I might be though I can't say so for sure, never having seen me own face owing to the difficulty of standing in front of meself for a good look.'

'Maybe you're a prince under an enchantment from a wicked witch, and if a princess kisses you three times you'll turn back to your real handsome self?' asked the Princess hopefully.

'Maybe I am but I don't remember it, your Grace,' said Evan.

'Of course you wouldn't! That must be it! I have a plan. I'll just kiss you three times and then you'll be strong and handsome, and clever and handsome, and we'll be married and live happily ever after and we'll have half my father's kingdom and when my father dies we'll have the lot. Won't that be fun?'

'Well, your Ladyship . . .,' began Evan dubiously, but he was too late. Before you could say 'plynlimmon' the tall Princess had puckered up, bent down, turned her head sideways so her nose wouldn't get in the way, and kissed him three times.

Nothing happened for a moment, then the Princess turned into a frog with a long nose and an unhappy expression and she no longer had long hair to hide her face behind. In fact she had no kind of hair at all. Not a hair to the lot of her, there wasn't. She began to hop up and down in one place, croaking dismally. Evan was horrified. He hastily picked her up and tucked her under his hat where she would be safe from being trodden under his iron boots. He turned and went back to the big cave where he had left Fletcher, the reformed ogre.

Fletcher was digging around in a big chest he had dragged from the remote deeps of the cave.

'There's lots of gold here you know, Evan bach,' he said cheerfully, 'More than enough for the two of us to share. Why, with this money I'll have no trouble bribing the clerks and porters at Oxenford to let me in, and before all the rest is spent with eating and drinking and lodging and buying ink I'll be Professor Fletcher and maybe even get to be Archbishop of Canterbury.'

'What's gold?' asked Evan simply.

'Gold? Well, you said my brother owed you five pieces of silver. One little piece of this gold is worth many pieces of silver. Why is your hat jumping up and down?'

'Ah, now, that must be the excitement,' said Evan, dragging it firmly down so that his great ears were pushed out on the sides of his head. 'Well, your Reverence, I'll just take some of this gold and be off because I feel that me mam might be worrying about me.'

'By all means,' said Fletcher airily. 'Here, take this lot.'

He handed Evan a big, leather sack, and the lad

Many Kinds of Magic

swung it up and over his shoulder.

'By the way, what happened to the Princess? Did you let her go free?' asked Fletcher.

'In a manner of speaking I did, and then again I didn't,' said Evan. 'Now it must be a fond farewell and a long goodbye, friend Fletcher, as me mam says. It's time I was going for the dragon has gone, your brother has gone, the Princess is going and so are you. You're a good ogre and I'll remember you for always when you get to be Pope of Rome.'

Fletcher blushed and looked embarrassed but you could see he was pleased for all that. Evan walked out carrying the bag of gold and turned his face towards home. But after a while, when he had felt a few little struggles under his hat, he stopped and said to himself, 'Evan boy, your mam would never forgive you if you didn't leave things tidy and there's no doubt that the King will be worrying and fretting and not sleeping well of nights thinking of his poor daughter and her fate. You better take her back to her castle, and see if you can ease the poor man's mind, boyo.'

With that he turned back and went to the town where he had been hired that morning. It was shut for the night, but by shouting he learned the way to the palace from a sentry he woke on the ramparts. He trotted along all night with his sack clinking on his back and his boots clonking on his feet and by daylight he had come to the King's castle, with the moat of green water round it. The frog had slept most of the journey, but when he lifted his hat and took her from between his ears she woke. When she saw the castle she began to leap around, and from her croaking and trying to bite him, Evan could guess she was upset about something.

'Ah, don't be taking on so, your Eminence,' he said. 'I'll just give you a little bathe and a brush-up before you go and see your kinfolk.' He took her gently by the hind foot and dunked her up and down in the cold water of the moat. 'There's not many boys from the mountains can say they've bathed a princess,' said Evan. 'There you are then,' he went on, shaking the frog dry. 'It didn't hurt a bit and you look as fresh as a little green flower now, as me mam used to say to me when I was but a little gosling and didn't want to bathe and she would do it for me most gentle.'

He hid his sack among the bulrushes and carried the frog gently to where the men-at-arms were lowering the drawbridge for the day. They heard him coming by the clanking of his iron boots and the happy song that sprang from his throat, for what Welshman wouldn't sing like a throstle on such a bright, happy morning.

The Captain of the Guard who was supervising the drawbridge that morning happened to be the one who had taken off the Three Black Brothers of Aberystwith when Evan had encountered them, so he knew the lad and was kindly disposed to him.

'Hello, lad,' he cried. 'What have you there so green on the palm of your right hand?'

'Well, I've brought back your Princess, though she's in a great fixing in that a witch seems to have been at her and turned her into a frog for now.'

'Are you sure?' asked the Captain.

'Haven't I been travelling all night to bring her home where she can be among her own folk that love

Many Kinds of Magic

her, with me legs dropping off with weary miles and me stomach as empty as a saddlebag?'

'Maybe you better come in and see the King, then,' said the Captain.

Evan clanged across the drawbridge and clonged on the courtyard cobblestones to the old man with the gold crown standing on the steps of the keep.

'I've brought your daughter home to you, your Excellency, seeing it was too far for the poor girl to hop for herself,' explained Evan, handing the frog to the King. 'There's some enchantment at her, I think.'

'If this is my daughter, I hope you don't plan on getting half the kingdom for her like I promised. She's not in a good way, I'd say, from looking at her. Maybe it's not my daughter you have here, maybe it's some other princess you've got hold of by mistake.'

'I got her from Thug the Ogre,' said Evan calmly. 'And if your Lordship would take a look at her nose you'd see what's what in a minute! Anyway, I don't want half your kingdom, what good would that be to me? No, your Exaltation, I'll settle for the free run of your kitchen and a bag of vittle to take with me on the lonely long rough road back to me own home where me mam's waiting for me.'

The King looked down at the frog on his palm. It was croaking excitedly, pointing at Evan and leaping around all over the place. 'Poor Izzabelle, you can see how excited she is at seeing her old father again!' said the King. The frog turned a kind of pinkish green and almost growled with frustration. 'Look, I think she is trying to thank you!'

'Her being happy and a good feed or three is reward

enough for a simple fellow like me,' said Evan smugly. 'Now if your Kindliness wouldn't mind pointing me feet in the direction of a cauldron of oatmeal porridge and a slab of boiled bacon and a loaf or two, with maybe a bucket of milk, I'd feel rewarded enough,' said Evan hopefully.

'You shall have all that, and bread and cheese to carry with you when you leave, humble, low-bred man,' said the King. 'Oh, by the way. Did the witch give any sort of hint about what might restore my lovely Izzabelle to her own sweet self again?'

Evan frowned and beckoned the King to come close so he could whisper in his ear privately.

The King's eyebrows shot up in surprise, and he was heard to say, 'Are you quite sure? Fancy that! A prince, it has to be? Well, I might find one soon, there's more of them round in the hills these past few years than there used to be. Now my boy, go and enjoy your breakfast. Here! Mess John! See this lad has his hunger satisfied.' So saying he swept away into the keep carrying the frog on his hand.

Evan spent a happy hour making free with the salt meat and the fresh meat, the boiled and baked and stewed meat in the castle kitchen, then took up a heavy sack of food and left, bowing humbly to all he passed. The Captain was nailing a big sign over the gate of the drawbridge as he went out. It read:

WANTED—ONE PRINCE. FOR PLEASANT EVENING EMPLOYMENT. GOOD REWARD AND LIGHT DUTIES. APPLY WITHIN.

Many Kinds of Magic

So Evan went home to his mam only a few days after he had left, carrying a bag of gold and an empty sack with a few crumbs in the bottom. His mam saw his short, thick figure coming up the mountain and sighed, for she had missed him.

When he got to the doorstep she pulled his head down by the ears and kissed him in welcome.

'I'm glad to see you safe home, boy,' she said. 'How did you find the world, now you have seen it?'

'It's a fine place, mam, you wouldn't believe the adventures I've had and the kindly, clever, generous folk I met. There was a man who fed me well, and a man who gave me a dry bed to sleep in. There was a kindly ogre who filled a sack with gold for us to spend, and a princess who didn't think much of me looks but her father was a kind man. And oh, mam, there was a little red girl dragon, and words can't tell the beauty of her with her wings, flying among the stars. But east, west, home's best is a true saying, I think, and we'll just live here happily ever after, now.'

So they did.

BRAVE SOLDIER LI WU

Li Wu was a young man who fled from the famine in Shantung Province after all his family had perished from hunger. He came at last to the city of Jilin in the north-east, and there found work as a groom of chariot horses in the household of the Provincial Governor. Here he was paid little money, but supplied with clothing, food and a corner of the stables where he could sleep. Because he had known such misery and sorrow in his short life this seemed a sanctuary to him. Here he became friendly with another young man named Wang Shan who had also lost all his relatives, and they grew to feel they were truly brothers. They shared all they had.

Wang Shan had heard the old people say, 'East of the Pass there are three treasures'. He did not know what two of these might be, but he knew the third treasure was the root of the ginseng plant which has sincere and affable qualities. It brings long life and cures all sickness. His dream was to become a ginseng hunter in the Ch'ang-Pai Mountains, yet he could never hope to get enough money to buy the food and tools to keep him through the summer while he sought the plant. So the two young men worked at grooming and caring for the swift, fierce horses and lived as best they might in the stables of the Governor.

One day the Duke from the neighbouring province came to visit Jilin. Horses were harnessed to chariots for a great hunting party to celebrate his visit. Li Wu and Wang Shan were ordered to be of the party to care for the horses. The bright cavalcade went to wild parts of the mountains which were not settled at that time. Those who lived on the plains below said the mountains were full of 'black bears that would eat your face, tigers that would rend you and droves of wild boars who could crunch your head like a nut!' These were the animals the Duke and the Governor intended to hunt.

Li Wu had practised secretly with a borrowed bow and had become a fine archer. Now he was ordered to be one of the beaters who had to shout their way through the thickets waving fiery torches to drive the wild beasts where the nobles waited to shoot. The horses Li Wu tended and loved had been harnessed to the Duke's chariot. As the line of men reached the edge of the forest; shouting, beating upon iron pots and waving their torches; a great tiger sprang from the bushes and leapt upon one of the horses of the Duke's team. The horse screamed and reared in pain and terror, upsetting the chariot and spilling the Duke upon the ground. Li Wu was frantic with worry at seeing the horse he loved so wounded. He snatched a bow from a soldier and shot an arrow that pierced the tiger's side till only the feathers showed.

Many Kinds of Magic

Then he dropped the bow and ran forward, snatching a torch from another man and thrusting it into the animal's face until it snarled and died.

The Duke was pleased with his bravery. He said, 'This groom is like Shu in the Book of Odes:

> *Through thickets and marshes flare the beater's*
>   *fires,*
> *Shu strips to the waist and holds a tiger down*
> *To bring pleasure to his Lord.*
> *The Marquis smiles and frowns; says,*
> *Don't try that again. I need men like you.'*

He gave Li Wu three pieces of silver for a present and wished to employ him but the Governor said he could not go. He, too, admired bravery and decreed that, henceforth, Li Wu should be a soldier in his bodyguard.

When Li Wu had been armed and dressed in his uniform he learned the drill, weapon-skill and salutes to fit him for his new duties. Though he had received advancement for his merit, yet he still remained firm in his friendship with Wang Shan. They sought each other out and spoke together often of their hopes and dreams as young men will.

When the snow had vanished at the end of Winter Li Wu said, 'Younger Brother, take this silver and buy yourself food. Now you can become a ginseng hunter and stay in the mountains seeking the precious root. You may make your fortune, one "old man" mountain ginseng sells for more than its weight in gold.'

'But this is your money,' said Wang Shan.

'I am now a soldier and some think me brave, yet, Younger Brother, to you only I say that it was to help the horse I fought, not to help the Duke. Therefore the money does not matter. Take it. It would make me glad to see you become rich.'

Wang Shan thought about this, then making the appropriate bow of respect he said, 'Elder Brother, I will take the money and go to the mountains. If the Gods permit, I shall return in the Autumn with many large ginseng, and any profit from their sale will be equally divided. That's fair, isn't it?'

Next morning he went to the market and bargained for salt, oil and millet, also for such tools as are needed for hunting the rare herb and carefully digging it from the earth. At the market he met a band of other men, true ginseng seekers who had been to the mountains many times. They agreed to let him come with them and to teach him the trade for a sum of money. When all were ready they slung their packs on their backs, took up their carrying poles of bamboo and set off for the peaks that loomed in the eastern sky.

This was very dangerous country. Even experienced mountaineers sometimes became lost and died in the pathless wilderness. If they went astray and their footsteps led them into such mystifying places as those called 'Dry Rice Bowl' and 'Empty Sauce Jar' then the maze of cliffs and thick forest made it impossible to get out again. The bones of many ginseng hunters lay whitening in the thickets, playthings for the wild beasts of the mountains.

The others quickly instructed Wang Shan in his new trade. They were honest, honourable men. Yet as weeks went by and no ginseng was found some felt that Wang Shan was the reason for their bad luck. At last the leader said to him, 'We are going away to another part of the mountains where we have dreamed that ginseng may be found. The men beg that you do not accompany us, they fear you have brought a curse with you that afflicts your companions. Therefore it is our wish that you do not come with us. We have found many roots here in the past, perhaps you will be successful.' Then they packed their loads, left him food, and went away.

Wang Shan was not too disturbed by this. He went on seeking the red flowers of the shy plant. He found one small ginseng worth as much money as he had spent on food and tools, so he was not unhappy. He would rise before daylight, prepare simple food of grain and wild herbs boiled together and begin his search as soon as it was light enough. Yet ginseng grows only in secret places. He searched for many days and found no more. Each evening he would play a little on his bamboo flute before going to sleep.

One evening as he was playing his favourite tune, 'Willows in Spring', someone came to the outer edge of the firelight to listen to the music. Whoever it was seemed very shy. Wang Shan pretended not to notice and went on playing as if he was alone. The stranger became bolder as time went by and one night came close enough for him to see. It was a small girl-child, dressed in a red apron. He bowed to her, for he was almost sure she was a mountain spirit; and kept playing the flute and made no other movement in case she should become nervous and flee. By the time the first Winter storms were due the spirit child was so sure of being safe that she would come right into the firelight and sit to listen to the music.

The time came when Wang Shan knew he could not stay safely in the mountains any longer. The wild geese had flown south, the cranes were gone, frost sparkled on the ground each morning and the nights were cold. Winter was almost upon him. He packed the little food he had remaining, barely enough to last him home; carefully wrapped the ginseng in its container of pine bark and prepared to leave next dawn for the plains.

That night when the spirit girl came to the fire he bowed gracefully and said, speaking to her for the first time, 'It is time for farewells. Tomorrow this humble person must leave the mountains. I will now play the tune 'Friends Going Away' for us. I feel we have become real friends. Thank you for the company you have brought me in the lonely days now ending.' He played the music sweetly and sadly. The little girl wept and bowed also before vanishing while he slept.

Next morning Wang Shan set out with light baskets slung from the pole and sadness in his heart. He had hoped to bring back riches for Li Wu, and he had only enough to pay for his keep during the Winter and for food enough to set out the next year. As he descended a steep crag he met the men who had taught him his trade. They were happy for they had found some of the precious plant; enough to let them spend the Winter in comfort. They greeted him happily and all set off homeward together.

As they reached the foothills and came to pathways made by men they quickened their pace. Wang

Shan was at the rear of the line, swinging his baskets from the pole and joining in the chant they sang to keep time as they jogged along. Suddenly there was a great roaring from a berry thicket beside the path and a huge bear sprang out and seized Wang Shan. He strove to draw his sharp knife to defend himself and his companions ran back to help him, but the bear killed him with a stroke of its thick arm and fled into the trees.

His friends sadly performed the rites and buried his body. They took his small belongings and when they reached Jilin to sell their ginseng they took the things to Li Wu and told him of the sad fate of his Younger Brother. They were honest men. They had sold his ginseng; now they gave Li Wu the money and the few possessions.

At first he wept bitterly at their news, but presently his face turned red with rage then white with passion. He opened the bundle and took out the flute. 'I will keep this in memory of the one who has passed upward,' he said. 'I will use the money to buy the finest weapons. I will not rest until I have killed this monster. Please share the rest of these things among yourselves, to keep in his memory.'

The ginseng hunters were much affected by his grief and rage, and the leader said, 'Thank you. We will make offerings for him, so he will know his companions have not forgotten him since he Went Above. But you must keep his knife, for that is the chief possession of a seeker of the "wonderful plant".' They then made their respects to Li Wu and departed in sorrow.

Whenever his duties allowed during the time of

snow Li Wu practised with his weapons. By the time of 'running melt-water' he had become thoroughly proficient. Upon the day he determined to ask the Governor for permission to depart on his hunt a deputation arrived from the farmers of the plain below the mountains. A monster bear was raiding the villages, killing men, women and children and destroying the crops. People were afraid to go out to plough for the Spring sowing, and crouched in their huts with barred doors. The Chief Headman begged the Governor to restore safety to the black-haired people of the plains. When the man had ended speaking, Li Wu stepped forward, knelt, bowed low three times and looked at the Governor in silence. Having permission to speak, he said, 'Lord, I beg of you to appoint me to this task. I am sure this is the same bear that killed my Younger Brother.'

The Governor was pleased with his boldness of spirit and remembered that this was the fellow who had attacked the tiger. He decided that Li Wu was the man to perform this dangerous task, for his anger would serve to keep him filled with the spirit of perseverance. 'Your request is granted! You shall be supplied with a quiver-full of iron-piercing arrows and the famous lance called Great Thrust. The people of the villages shall sustain you with shelter and food while you search for this monster. Return victorious!' Then he dismissed them all.

Li Wu went with the villagers. His heart was full of courage, his eyes burned with red fire. He was like Second Brother Juan in *The Men Of The Marshes*, of whom it was said: 'Features like a cliff-face, brown hair tangled on his chest, thick shoulders, arms of strength to lift mountains.'

The villagers led Li Wu past the districts of Dunhua and Jiaoho to their own villages. They cared for him and fed him with their best food and oldest wine. He would rise before dawn and hunt all day, or roam restlessly and silently all the dark hours, armed and savage, eating and drinking little. Though he travelled thus through the whole of the plains yet still he could not find the killer. Despite his sincere efforts the bear would always strike in a place where he was not. At last he thought of another plan, so called the Chief Headman to him.

'This is no ordinary bear,' he told the man when he met him. 'This is a spirit creature who has broken the laws of its kind and been cast out by the other bears. Something seems to warn it of me. I will go into the forest and find its lair. Then I may be able to bring it to battle.'

The villagers were afraid for his safety if he went into the mountains where so many had been lost. But Li Wu was a true Brave, one who would dare even death itself. They saw his determination and, sighing, they gave him food and advice and watched his strong figure climb the steep path to the wilderness.

Li Wu hunted through the tangle for some days; scaling high cliffs, leaping over chasms and descending precipices. By chance he came to the region where Wang Shan had sought ginseng, and there he camped for the night. He took the bamboo flute from his pack and began playing 'Willows in Spring', his Younger Brother's favourite tune. Tears glistened on his cheeks as he remembered their friendship. He was startled when a young girl appeared in the firelight and said, 'Who are you who plays the flute of my friend Wang Shan? What has become of him?'

Li Wu saw straight away that this was no ordinary girl-child. Her skin was coloured like old ivory and smooth as fine jade. She wore a red apron and there were two gold pins in her hair. He stopped playing at once and bowed low.

'This person is named Wu, of the family Li. I came to the mountains to seek revenge for the death of my friend Wang Shan, cruelly killed last Autumn by a devil shaped as a bear.'

The child began to weep also, and sat upon a tree-trunk in the firelight.

'If you were Wang Shan's friend then you must be an honourable man,' she said. 'He was my friend also, for he was gentle and kind. It was my intention to reward him for his patience and cheerfulness when he returned this Summer. Let us grieve for him together. Play the tune "Friends Going Away" for his memory on his flute, for that was the last music he played here; and I will mourn for him while you play.' So together they remembered him in a seemly way.

When the music and mourning were over the girl said, 'Tell me about his death.'

'It was a great bear, one who has also killed many farmers and wives and children on the plains and destroyed their crops. The Governor has decreed that it must die so the peace of the Sublime Emperor can be maintained.'

'That is the bear named "Strong Arm",' said the spirit child. 'I know its hiding-place and will lead you there; though I fear it will slay you also, Elder

Brother. Be advised, return to the capital and get men to help you or you will perish. It is powerful, savage and fearless!'

'I have given my iron word not to return until it is dead or else it has slain me,' said Li Wu calmly. 'In the name of the friendship you bore my brother, tell me where to find the beast.'

'I will whisper when the day returns, since you are determined,' said the child, and vanished in a strange way.

Next morning Li Wu rose before light to polish his armour and sharpen his weapons. He took no food with him, having faith that the child would be true to her word. When the sun rose he began fearlessly walking through the deep thickets taking no care to hide the sound of his passing. Indeed he called aloud as he went, challenging the bear. Whenever he came to a clear place the sun glinted on his breast-plate so it twinkled like a star, lighting up his ruddy cheeks, resolute countenance and short, thick bow. Tigers watched him pass respectfully and droves of wild boars made a passage for him through their ranks. In mid-morning a soft voice whispered in his ear, 'Climb the spur to your right hand. He is there in his den, asleep.'

Li Wu turned in the ordained direction and climbed the steep slope, leaping boulders and smashing bushes aside. He found the narrow, dark mouth of a cave. Placing his lance to hand, he took the bow and sped many swift arrows into the cave like swallows. There came a terrifying roar from within and soon a great shaggy bear rushed blinking into the light with four arrows piercing its coat. Its relentless eyes glared to where Li Wu was still fear-lessly shooting, arrow after arrow, then it opened awful jaws and charged downhill toward him.

Coolly he fired again at its breast as it came closer. When it rose from all fours and stood with enormous arms outstretched to grasp he dropped the bow and took up the lance, keen and bright and deadly as a venomous serpent. Li Wu charged the bear and thrust the lance into the bear's breast next to the arrows.

The bear screamed pain and fury and launched itself upon him, smiting him with its dirty claws so his face was scored and smitten and blood flowed down like a river on to his shoulder and breastplate. Yet he held firm to the lance, placing the butt against a rock that protected his back. The bear thrust toward him again, and now this forced the blade deeper and deeper into its thundering heart. It fell forward in death, crushing Li Wu beneath its stinking hair and breaking his arm. Blinded by his own blood, he somehow freed his good arm, drew Wang Shan's knife and drove it into the dead body of his huge opponent. 'This is for Wang Shan!' he shouted fiercely before fainting with pain.

When he woke he found his body-armour had been removed and a piece of cloth was bound across his torn face. His arm was tied in the recognized way so the bones would set straight, and he was more comfortable than he had hoped. He was terribly thirsty, parched and dry and he gasped for water. The girl appeared, this time wearing only a simple robe, for she had used the apron to bind his cheeks where the bear had ripped them. The apron had healing virtue, he was sure, for he felt less pain than he expected.

The girl gave him sips of water from a birch-bark container, then said, 'Your sworn word is accomplished. Our brother's shade can rest. Now he sees the shade of his murderer behind him and will be comforted. Meantime, I can help you further, Tiger Warrior.'

She took his dagger and cut off four of the small, pink toes from her foot. These she slipped into his mouth. He tasted a miraculous flavour. She said, 'Wash them down with water.' He did so and immediately felt strong and happy. To his surprise he saw she had grown new toes straight away. Then he knew she was a ginseng spirit, not a human child at all.

'You will soon be well, for my body has marvellous power,' she said, 'What will you do then?'

'Take this bearskin to the Governor to show I have kept faith,' said Li Wu. 'Then I think I will no longer be a soldier. Since eating the ginseng my spirit has changed inside me. I no longer wish to live in streets and between houses, or to gain fame and merit as a warrior. I will return to these mountains and consider the Great Truths.'

'So, your heart is changed. It is said of me, "much healing, many changes", and a change has taken place. We will be friends from now on,' said the child, and she left him to sleep his pain away.

When he woke he found his wounds completely healed and his arm-bones knitted straight and strong. He removed the apron from his face and went to the nearest stream to wash the dried blood from his face and body where it glistened like lacquer. In the mirror of the placid water he saw his face was completely healed, though terribly scored and scarred by the huge talons that had slashed him. However he felt vigorous and young. He carefully washed the apron in the water and hung it on a bush to dry where the ginseng-child would find it. Then he took his dagger and skinned the bear. Leaving the carcass to feed the foxes and birds, he rolled his armour and weapons in the heavy skin and took the bundle on his shoulder. Then he set out for the nearest of the villages on the plains, feeling no exhaustion despite his heavy burden and the steep ways.

When he reached the village he ordered the skin to be dressed and tanned, and his armour and weapons be cleaned and polished. The villagers received him with awe, seeing the marks of the bear on his face and shoulders. They wanted to feast him, but all he would eat was a little plain food and all he would drink was tea. When he was assured that all was ready, he commanded a cart to carry the skin. He returned to Jilin accompanied by the Chief Headman and two others to drive the cart and tend the animals that pulled it. He walked ahead in ordinary clothes, saying he would no longer wear the armour of a fighting man.

The Governor was holding court when the little procession arrived and they were admitted at once. Li Wu entered first, bearing his weapons and armour. These he laid upon the ground before the Governor. He bowed three times, very deeply, as the villagers carried in the enormous skin and rolled it out for all to see. All gasped at the size.

The Governor rose to examine it, then resumed his chair of office. He stared keenly at the face of Li Wu, and said, 'You have done well, soldier. Your face shows that it was not an easy task. In reward you may ask a favour and if it is possible, it shall be granted.'

Li Wu knelt and beat his forehead upon the flag-stones. 'One favour only, Lord,' he said. 'Release me so I can go free to live as I wish, quietly in the mountains. The "Cold Mountain Poet" said:

> High in a labyrinth of mountains
> Only the birds have paths
> Clouds are the fields I till and harvest,
> All the long years – I forget how many.
> Seasons come and go,
> Watching them pass I think:
> Tell this to people who seek money,
> What's the use of it all?

'You see, the mountains have entered into me and now I wish to enter into the mountains.'

The Governor was an enlightened man. He looked at the deep scars on the brave man's cheeks and neck, and yet underneath he seemed to see a glow which had not been there previously. He said:

> Who can cut the strings
> Binding him to the world
> To sit among white clouds?

Then he granted Li Wu his wish and released him, yet he saw the Chief Headman of the villages of the plain privately before he dismissed him.

Having great reverence for Li Wu, the farmers took food and left it for him in the hills. Sometimes it would vanish, sometimes not. After many years no one ever heard again of Li Wu in the Ch'ang-Pai Mountains. But a new kind of bird appeared, sometimes seen and heard by the ginseng gatherers of the wilderness. They named it the 'ginseng bird'. They say if you hear it call in the valleys or on the slopes of the mountains and follow its calling you will often find ginseng. It is their friend and they will not allow anyone to harm it. They say it is married to the ginseng spirit and the two are never far from each other.

Whether this is true or not, there is a bird in the Ch'ang-Pai's and as it flies from peak to peak or along the valleys, its voice can be heard calling, 'Li Wu! Li Wu! Li Wu!'

# How FIRE CAME

Once on a time a very long time ago the people didn't have any fire. They had to eat all their food raw, there was no way to cook it. They had no way to keep warm in winter when the wind from the south-west blew its cold breath, frosting the grasses and making even the branches of the trees shiver with the cold. The people had nothing but their skin cloaks, and these weren't really enough, especially in the dark nights. The wicked Things that travel on the night winds found that the people were easy to catch and torment, there was no fire to frighten them away. The old men did their best using their songs of power, but this meant that they didn't get much sleep because they had to be always on the alert to protect the people.

One of the clever men of this tribe was named Gud-ah. He was a very clever fellow but also he was selfish and miserly. One day he took shelter under a tree during a great thunderstorm, and the tree was struck by lightning. The power of the lightning entered the wood of the tree and set it on fire. When Gud-ah felt the warm air from the fire on his skin he thought, 'What a wonderful thing this is! It feeds on the dead wood like the kangaroo feeds on the grass, and it brings comfort to me. I like this thing; I think I'll just keep it.'

The other people of the tribe noticed that every night from then on Gud-ah went off by himself to camp. Sometimes they smelt delicious smoke of cooking meat that made their mouths fill with sweet water. 'What's this? What's this good smell we have never smelt before?' they asked each other.

But Gud-ah wouldn't answer when they asked him about it. He just said, 'Oh, that's something that belongs to me.'

Now, those old men were clever. You can't hide anything from them, they always find out about everything. Soon they found out that Gud-ah had fire. He was cooking his food, and he was keeping himself warm. He was able to sleep all night because the bad Things that fly on the dark winds were afraid of the fire, and so didn't trouble him. The old men went to Gud-ah and said, 'This is a good thing you've got there! Give some to us. We'd like a bit of it so we can feed it on dead wood, too, and do all the good things you are doing.'

Gud-ah said, 'No. This is mine. I'm going to keep it for myself. And don't try to take it, because I've put a singing spell around the fire and it can't go out from where it is.' So he wouldn't give any of his fire to them.

The old men went away and talked about it. They could put the killers on to Gud-ah, but he was a great warrior and some of the killers would be killed. His magic stopped anybody from coming along and taking a burning piece of wood from the side of the fire. They didn't know what to do. But one old man, another clever man, said, 'I'll fix him, just leave it to me.'

He sang a magic song, and a big whirlwind came along, swaying and dancing across the ground the way they do. It couldn't get the fire from the side, because Gud-ah's spell stopped it, so it jumped its tail over the top and descended on to the fire. It quickly sucked up all the embers and burning sticks and whirled them aloft. Then it danced away across the plain, dropping a bit of fire here and a bit there so that little fires sprang up everywhere, and all the families were able to get some.

The people were very happy then, because the children didn't shiver all night any more. They were able to grill their fish and eels they caught, and roast the kangaroos instead of having to eat them raw. Best of all for the old men, they didn't have to sit up all night any more to keep the bad Things away, and the only people who got caught by Them were the silly ones who broke the law and went away into the dark by themselves. Everybody laughed at Gud-ah, because they had given him a trick, and he got very angry and went away to live in the hills by himself, where the white man calls the Black Range.

The old men knew that Gud-ah would try to get his pay-back revenge on them, and take the fire away. They knew they hadn't heard the last of it. They sat every night talking about what they might do to keep the fire for the people in spite of him, but they couldn't think of a proper plan for a long time. But at last the same old man who had sung the magic whirlwind had an idea, and told the others.

'Gud-ah is a rainmaker, you all know that. Perhaps he's going to make a big rain and put the fires out so they can't be lit again. I'll tell you what we can do. You all know the little bats, that live in the hollows of the dead trees? I can turn us into those little bats, they're magic, you know, they're the Messengers. They can catch spirit things. When we are all bats, we can catch the spirit part of fires, the part that lives in the lightning. We can hide that spirit in the dead wood of the trees. Then when the fires go out we'll be able to get it back from the wood and start the fires again.'

The other old men thought this was a good idea, and that's what they did. They turned into little bats, and they took the spirit of fire and hid it in the wood of the dead trees.

Gud-ah was sitting in the hills, and he was planning to hurt the people.

He took his magic rainstones from his bag, and he sang them so that rain began to gather in the clouds overhead. He sang and sang so that more and more came. Soon there was a great big lot of rain in the clouds, and when he let it all go it was like a water-fall all over the Plains. The water put all the fires out in all the camps, and Gud-ah chuckled to himself as he watched from the highest part of the mountains. When the rain was all over, no sign of smoke reaching into the sky could be seen anywhere. All the fires were out.

That night a great wind came from the west and blew on the land so everything dried out. Gud-ah was still on top of his mountain, and he looked and

Many Kinds of Magic

looked. What's that! Here and there, across the Plains, little coils of smoke had started to rise. The people had got their fires back.

As soon as the land had dried, the old men had turned back to themselves once more. Each went to a dead tree and took a piece of dried wood. They called the men to them and said, 'Take a piece of soft wood like this and put it on the ground. Now get a stick of hard wood with a pointed end, and spin it on the soft wood. See, it gets hot, it starts to smoke. Now it catches the dry grass we have ready! The spirit of the fire is in the wood, it doesn't matter if the fires go out, we can always get them back again now!'

So the people could always make fire from then on. Gud-ah was so angry he went away and they never heard anything about him again after that.

POOR JOSE

High on the Altiplano of the Andes Mountains lived a poor man named Jose. He was a farmer, but he did not own any land of his own. His fat cousin Jaime, who lived in a real house in the town in the valley far below, allowed Jose to grow crops on a fine piece of land he owned but was too lazy to work for himself. Jose was famous for growing the finest potatoes for hundreds of kilometres around. He chose the plants carefully, dug the land deep and fine and kept the plants weeded clean while they were growing.

Once a year Jaime would climb to the farm with his beasts of burden for Jose to load after the harvest. Then he would take all the crops to the market in the town to sell them. When he had the money he would hide most of it in his iron chest where he kept his wealth, and take only a little share back to Jose.

Jose wanted a bigger, fairer share of the money. He wanted to save enough to buy land of his own. He thought it was fair that he ought to get half the money at least because it was he who did all the work. Jaime would not give him more. The first year his excuse was that potatoes had been very plentiful and that he had got only a little money for them. The next year he said that most of the potatoes had rotted from a disease leaving few fit to sell. But the third year he could think of no more excuses, and so he told Jose that it was his fine land that grew the potatoes, after all, and that all Jose had to do was put them in the earth and watch them grow, therefore he was entitled to almost all the money. Cunning Jaime! He knew that if ever Jose saved enough to buy his own farm he would not work for his cousin and more! So it went, each year Jaime grew fatter and lazier, and every year Jose grew thinner and more wrinkled and bent from long hours of hard work.

At the end of harvest the fourth year Jaime was puffing up the steep mountain track leading his beasts to load the crops when he came upon a small llama caught in thorny bushes near the edge of a precipice. The little creature bleated piteously for help but Jaime looked at the towering rocks and the deep gulf below, and trembled with fear. 'No, no, beast! You got yourself into trouble, now you must get yourself out again,' he said importantly and panted by on his way to the farm on the high, rugged plateau.

Once there he again cheated Jose of his share of the money, making excuses and pretending that he was doing a kindness by letting him do all the hard work. When the animals were loaded he went off with them, but he forgot his tobacco-pouch. Jose found it soon after the caravan had left and ran down the hillside after him to return it, for he was an honest man. He caught up with Jaime near the foot of the path, but got only a grunted word of thanks for his kindness.

On his way back to the heights Jose came upon the same small llama Jaime had seen. It bleated hoarsely for it was very thirsty and hungry by now, worn out by its struggle to escape.

'Poor little one,' said Jose compassionately. 'Wait, wait, soon I will return and save you!' He ran uphill to his lowly hut and came back with a coil of rope. He fastened one end of this to a great boulder and tied the other around his waist. Carefully he lowered himself to where the llama was trapped. He patiently unhooked the curving thorns from its woolly coat, freed it, took it in his arms and carried it back to the path. He gave it a drink from his own water-skin, and stayed with it while it rested until it was almost recovered.

'Go, little one,' he said at last. 'Resume your play upon the hills and among the wild grasses. Be careful from now on and slip no more into danger!'

He coiled the rope, slung it across his shoulder, picked up the water-skin and began the long ascent home. To his amazement the llama followed and when he reached the little hut he found it was still with him. He fed and tended it, putting it into the corral for the night, but when he rose at dawn next day it was gone. It was most mysterious. The gates were closed, the rails unbroken, but the llama had vanished.

Jose did not mind. He was pleased the little beast had departed to take up its wild, free life again. But at noon, when he sat in the meagre shade at the edge of the field to rest while he ate corn-cake and drank water from his leather bottle, he was startled to see a beautiful woman coming across the deeply spaded field toward him. She was dressed in a beautiful embroidered robe and wore ornaments of gold and emeralds, any one of which would have bought him a fine farm, so precious were they. He stood, took off his hard black hat, and bowed respectfully for he could easily see this was no ordinary woman.

'You are Jose, the one who rescued a small llama yesterday?' she asked.

He bowed silently, being too nervous and shy to speak.

'It is my pet and I love it dearly. You shall have a reward. I have brought you this leather bag. If you keep it safely you will never go hungry or thirsty again, though you live a hundred years.'

He bowed again, but this time he gathered courage to look up into the lady's face. She smiled and held out a leather sack.

'Take this. Instead of cooking your dinner this evening, tap three times on the bag then loosen the string that keeps it closed. Then you will see what you will see!' She laid the bag upon the earth, smiled at him again, and vanished.

Jose thought he must be dreaming. When he looked at the soft, newly dug earth he could see no footprints! Yet the bag lay upon the ground where she had put it. Jose picked it up by the neck. It wasn't very heavy. Shaking his head he put down the bag, picked up his spade and began work again.

That evening at dusk when he got back to his little hut he was tired, almost too tired to bother cooking his food. He remembered what the lady had said. He

Many Kinds of Magic

took the bag, tapped it three times, and loosened the knotted leather thong that kept it sealed.

The bag became so heavy he was forced to set it on the floor.

Just as well he did! Two boys climbed from the sack carrying a golden table and a golden chair. They placed these upon the mud floor and beckoned Jose to sit down. When he overcame his shyness and was seated, they both dived into the sack again and emerged seconds later bearing the most tasty dishes of food and bottles of the most delicious wine. These they laid on the table in front of Jose. Then they stood behind his chair serving him. When his plate was almost empty they piled it high again; when he drank from his golden cup they immediately filled it for him again. At last he could eat no more.

'Thank you, thank you, I have had enough,' said Jose.

At once they gathered up the dishes and bottles and scraps and tossed them into the sack. They bowed low to Jose, took the table and chair and vanished into the sack themselves. It bulged and wriggled for a second then once more appeared to be empty. Jose peeped into the interior but there was nothing to show where the two boys might have gone.

He thoughtfully tied the leather thong around the neck of the sack again and hung it from a hook set into the mud wall. Feeling better fed and more comfortable than he had for years Jose went to his hard bed and slept soundly until a little glow in the sky over the snowy eastern peaks told him it was time to rise for another day's work. He washed his face and dried it, then turned to stir the fire, but it was out. Of course! He hadn't needed to build it up to cook his dinner the night before, and he had forgotten to put wood on it to keep it burning through the dark hours. Now he was shivering in the thin, chill air of the high plateau and was sorry for his forgetfulness. Quickly he kindled a blaze and was about to begin cooking his breakfast when he remembered the lady's words. He took the bag from its peg, tapped it three times, and unlaced the top.

The two boys sprang out again. This time they brought a wooden table and chair, finely carved with fruit and flowers. When he was seated they disappeared into the sack and quickly returned bearing fruit and meat and a bowl of cooked beans so hot with chillies that it seemed to steam in the cold air! Also they brought a boiling pot of the finest coffee. Jose ate the finest breakfast he had ever tasted.

So a new life began for him. He still worked in the fields from early till late; tilling the soil, planting maize and potatoes and hoeing them clean of weeds, but now he had a fine breakfast and a rich dinner without having to cook them or worry about washing the pots and platters. He grew strong and handsome again from the good food and hard work in the pure, cold mountain air. There seemed to be some virtue in the bag, some magic that was more than just food and comfort, for the crops grew better than ever they had before. The many ears of maize ripened to plumpness as the silk browned at the end of the ears, and the potatoes flowered and bore with profusion.

When Jaime came groaning up the mountain path with his beasts (groaning because he had become

Many Kinds of Magic

fatter than ever), Jose met him on the track to help. Jaime looked at him suspiciously. His eyes were merry and clear, his body strong and upright and his cheeks glowed with perfect health.

'You have been lazy!' shouted Jaime furiously. 'You have been eating *my* good food grown in *my* good ground instead of saving it to sell in the valley market!'

'Indeed I haven't cousin. See, here are many sacks of maize, here are many sacks of potatoes! All ready and ripened for you to take away. Look, the barn is filled!'

Jaime puffed into the mud-floored barn, and sure enough it was overflowing with the finest crop he had ever seen. The grains of maize were golden and round and plump and the potatoes were clean and ripe and mealy without blemish. He stared at Jose, but cunningly hid his suspicions and jealousy. He praised the virtues of his own fine land he allowed the simple farmer to till.

'The land is so good and fertile that my beasts will need help to get all this carried down the trail in one journey,' he said craftily. 'You might like to come down with me and help, dear cousin.'

'Of course I'll help you,' said Jose – honest, simple Jose, the good man of no cunning.

Together they loaded the animals; then Jaime led them off downhill while Jose followed carrying a great bag of maize on his broad shoulder. They travelled all afternoon, and by evening led the little procession of animals into the corral beside Jaime's fine house in the valley town. Jaime went inside to see his wife about a meal for them while Jose unloaded and stacked the produce and fed and tended the tired beasts. Just as he finished all the work Jaime came back and said, 'Alas, cousin, my wife did not expect you to come back with me. She has cooked only enough food for herself and me. I am sorry, but tonight I can give you no food!'

Jose smiled simply and said, 'Don't worry, dear cousin. I am used to hunger. I will hurry back to the farm in the morning, but tonight I will sleep fasting. Perhaps your wife will cook me some breakfast before I leave.'

'Goodnight, then,' said Jaime. 'Sleep lightly, you must guard the grain against thieves while you sleep in my fine barn.'

'Of course, of course cousin. All will be safe while I am here.'

When Jaime had departed to eat the food his wife had cooked, Jose smiled quietly and drew the magic sack from inside the front of his shirt where he had been carrying it. He tapped it three times, and out sprang the two boys. They set forth the table and chair and brought the most beautiful food and wine of the best. They bowed Jose to his chair as though he was some great official and took care his plate and cup were never empty. When he had said, 'Thanks, thanks. I have had enough!' they cleared away in an instant and things were as they had been before. Jose smiled with contentment and hung the sack upon a peg driven into the wall of the barn. Then he stretched himself out upon a pile of empty sacks and was soon snoring.

Jaime had gone into the house to eat, but like greedy people he had a keen nose for a cooking-pot smell. He became aware of a delicious odour wafting on the tiny breeze that came through the shutters of the window behind him. He followed his nose carefully and quietly toward the barn and there placed one eye to a crack in the timbers of the wall. Imagine his surprise when he saw his cousin eating and drinking like a great Governor, with two servants to wait upon him! Jaime stayed watching till Jose dismissed the boys into the bag, hung it on the wall, and went to sleep. Then the greedy fat man went into the house again and told his wife what he had seen.

'Ah!' he cried angrily. 'This miracle is wasted on one so dull and ignorant as my stupid cousin. If only we had that magic sack, wife! You would not have to cook or wash up any more, and we could save all the good money we are forced to pay for our food. Also we would have two servants and good wine!'

'Where is this bag now?' asked his cunning wife.

'Hanging upon a peg beside his head as he sleeps in the barn.'

'Husband, you slip out and bring the bag here without waking him. Here we have all sorts of leather and thread! I will sew another bag so like this magic one that the poor fool will not notice the difference. He is so stupid that he will only think it has lost its virtue. That's the way we can get this marvel for ourselves!'

'You are a treasure among wives,' said Jaime as he stole out to get the bag.

She carefully selected a piece of leather that seemed the same as the leather of the sack, and she sewed all that night by candle-light. Before dawn the new bag was ready. It was so craftily made it was impossible to tell it from the true one. Jaime took it to the barn and hung it on the wooden peg in place of the lady's gift. He was just in time, as he turned to go he saw Jose begin to stir.

He crept out, then returned noisily, banging the door and shouting, 'Come, cousin, dear cousin. My wife has cooked breakfast for you. You must eat and return to the farm, while I sell the grain and potatoes for us. Hurry, hurry; you have a long, steep trail ahead of you!'

Jose was grateful for the breakfast the greedy couple gave him, though it was not nearly so fine as he would have got from his magic bag. When he had eaten he stuffed the false sack into the front of his shirt and took the road out of the village and back to the high plains and the farm.

Jaime and his wife watched him go with secret glee. As soon as he was out of sight around the windings of the path they took the sack and soon discovered the secret and sat down to a dinner such as the greatest general in the land never enjoyed in his great white stone palace! From that day forward they grew fatter and fatter and lazier and lazier until they could hardly stir from their chairs.

Meantime, Jose had gone back to the farm under the snow-capped high peaks looming eternally in the east. That night, no matter how he rapped and rapped and tied and untied the bag no servants appeared. He was forced to cook a meagre dinner from worm-eaten corn-cobs and spotted potatoes. Then he stretched his tired body on his hard pallet and cried himself to sleep.

Some days later he sat sadly in the shade of the thorny hedge at noon, and was startled when the tall, beautiful lady appeared before him once more. Quickly he shuffled to his feet and took off his hard black hat, but he could not meet her eye as he waited for her to speak.

'So, Jose, how are you, kindly man? Has your cousin given you a fair share of the money for the crops this time? You should get a lot of money this year, for as well as all the hard work you did, I put my blessing on the ground and on the crops.'

Jose hung his head, for he was afraid to tell the lady what had happened. By now he had worked out in his mind what had happened and how Jaime must have stolen the bag, but he didn't know what to do about it.

The lady had keen eyes and soon saw that all was not well with him. She pressed him with questions until he confessed that his reward had been stolen from him and also that Jaime had not even given him a small share of the money from the crops. The lady was angry.

'You are a simple fool,' she snapped. 'You have let that cruel man who passed my little pet by when it was in danger take the reward I gave you for saving it! You are good man, Jose, but you are too good. Too gentle. But I will give you another magic bag. This one will be different, but if you learn to use your good head as well as you use your good heart perhaps you may save the bag your greedy cousin has stolen.'

She plucked another sack from empty air and handed it to Jose. It looked exactly like the first one she had given him. Jose thanked her humbly but she only smiled grimly and went off without another word.

He could hardly wait to get home, he was so hungry. Once he was safely inside the hut he tapped upon the bag three times, then loosened the thong. Out of the bag leapt two strong, blue devils with thick clubs; and with these weapons they banged Jose on the head and feet and front and back and sides until he was blue with bruises and his head ached terribly. He broke away from them at last and ran away shouting, 'Thank you, thank you. I have had enough!' The devils turned grumblingly away and went back into the bag and vanished. Trembling, Jose crept warily up to the sack and once more tied the thong around its neck so they could not get out again. Then he sat down to bathe his bruises with hot water and rub them with herbs.

Poor Jose, he wasn't very clever. At first he only wondered and complained that the lady should play such a trick on him. Then he remembered what she had said about using his head. What had she meant? Certainly it was aching enough from all the strokes it had got from the cudgels of the blue devils! Why should he be punished? It was not fair! He rested his aching head on his hands with his elbows on the table and thought. 'It would be fair if I had my old bag back and this one was for Jaime,' he thought resentfully. 'It is Jaime who deserves the beating. I have got the reward he earned, and he has got mine!'

Suddenly he had an idea. He had the bag Jaime should have got. Jaime had the bag he should have got! Perhaps this was what the lady had meant when she said he should begin using his head. Suppose, just suppose . . . .

Next morning he rose early and dressed himself in his fine clothes that he wore only to the fiestas. He felt much better, though his bones ached still from the beating they had the evening before. He took the new sack, stuffed it into the front of his shirt and walked off down the long twisting path toward the valley. He breathed the clean, pure air of the mountains into his sore ribs, glorying in its freshness. He walked with his head high, seeing the majesty of the snow-covered peaks, the blue sky reflected in the little lakes of melt-water and the tiny bright flowers that hid shyly among the boulders and broken rocks. By the time he had reached the bottom of the trail, dusk was falling. It was quite dark before he entered the town and made his way quietly to the home of Jaime.

He peeked through the window and saw Jaime take the sack from the wall, tap it three times and open it. Out sprang the two boys, bringing the table and chairs with them. They heaped the table with great platters of rich food and pitchers of fine wine for the greedy husband and wife. When they had begun eating Jose walked into the house without knocking or calling. He simply flung the door wide and walked in. The guilty pair were so astonished to see him they almost forgot to chew and swallow. Jose did not shout or show any anger, he simply greeted them warmly and sat on a chair.

'Blessings on this house and on you both, good cousin,' said Jose. 'So, you found the old sack I left, did you? I am glad for you! I am pleased you discovered the secret. Now you will never be hungry again.'

Jaime looked warily at him. 'Why have you come to visit us?' he asked suspiciously, not even rising to greet Jose. 'I hope you haven't come expecting to get a lot of money for your share of the crops my land grew for us. The market was bad. I didn't get much for all the maize and potatoes. There is no gold to share. Just a little silver.'

Jose pretended to laugh. 'Oh, you may keep that money, cousin. I don't need to work for gold any more since I got this new sack.' He took it from the front of his shirt and waved it carelessly in the air before him. 'Why, I can get all the gold I need in a minute from this magic bag. All the finest coins, bright, heavy gold! A man who can get gold does not bother about any old bag that brings only food. He can buy all the food he needs and have plenty left for anything else he needs. This new sack beats the old one altogether!'

'Will you stay the night with us, cousin of my husband!' asked the fat wife cunningly. 'We are so pleased to see you. Will you drink a little brandy? Will you share our humble meal?'

Jose pretended to be doubtful, while he considered this request. He seemed to hesitate.

'Yes, yes. Stay this night here and go on your way rested in the morning,' said Jaime hastily, guessing what his wife was planning.

'I am going down to the capital where I shall buy a great stone house,' said Jose importantly. 'Then I shall get the best furnishings and many servants, and perhaps find a beautiful girl who will want to marry

Many Kinds of Magic

such a rich man. When one has money one can no longer live so bare and cold a life as the high plains offer. No, indeed!'

'Of course, of course,' agreed his cousin. 'But family loyalty is such a beautiful thing, we are related, after all. Why, I might take the time to come with you and advise you in this matter, for I have been to the capital twice and so know all about it. Now, sit and talk, try a little brandy, and in the morning we will go on with a good heart.'

Jose pretended to let them persuade him, so they spent a merry evening, each made happier because he knew something the other did not. In the middle of the night Jose saw from his bed (where he was pretending to sleep), a line of candle-light appear under the door of the room where he lay. The door silently opened and in stole Jaime, carrying the magic food sack. He quickly unhooked the new sack from the wall, replaced it with the food bag and stole out again. As the light of the candle died away Jose grinned to himself, and then he turned over and really went to sleep.

Next morning fat Jaime woke Jose very early. 'Alas, cousin, I have had news that will keep me here today and so I cannot come with you to the capital. But my wife has cooked you a fine breakfast so you can be off early. Hurry, now.' Jose pretended to linger, stretching his arms and yawning, but at last when he had eaten he let the greedy pair hasten him through the door. He took the road leading to the coast and the capital and Jaime and his wife watched him go, waving and calling good wishes after him as he strode out of sight. When he could no longer see them round a bend in the road, Jose slipped the food sack safely into his shirt and made his way secretly back to the village. He wanted to see what happened when his cousin opened the sack! He hid behind a great boulder from where he could watch the street without being seen, and settled down to wait.

Presently he heard a loud screaming and shouting! The door of his cousin's house was flung wide and out tumbled Jaime and his fat wife, both being belaboured by blue devils! Off down the street they ran, out of sight and for all I know they are running still.

Jose laughed and laughed, rolling around in the dust behind his boulder. Then he rose, went to Jaime's house, and took a share of the money he found there, enough to repay all that Jaime had tricked from him in the years gone by. It was more than enough to let him buy a good piece of land for a farm and build a house on it with a proper wooden floor instead of beaten earth, and a roof that did not leak no matter how heavily the rain fell or how strongly the wind blew. He continued working as hard as ever he had done, and soon became prosperous. At last he married a farmer's daughter, who was not very beautiful but who was very strong and a willing worker, and who was happy and smiled all the time.

Some time after this the magic sack vanished one night but Jose was so happy with his farm and his wife and children that he didn't even notice at first, and only laughed about it when he did. So they lived happily, and so they do still.

ICE WOMAN

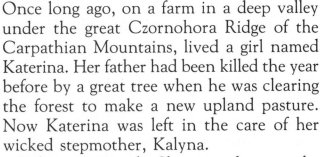

Once long ago, on a farm in a deep valley under the great Czornohora Ridge of the Carpathian Mountains, lived a girl named Katerina. Her father had been killed the year before by a great tree when he was clearing the forest to make a new upland pasture. Now Katerina was left in the care of her wicked stepmother, Kalyna.

Kalyna was greedy. She wanted to own the whole of the farm and all the animals; the fiery horses, the mild-eyed cattle, the silly sheep and the active goats. This greedy dream could not come true while Katerina lived. Kalyna was cowardly, as is often the case with cruel people. She knew that if the child died while under her care, the uncles and cousins would be suspicious and ask many questions. If they found her guilty she would be in reach of the iron teeth of justice. Therefore she planned and schemed to find a way to end Katerina's life so that no guilt would fall on her. In the meantime, she made her stepdaughter work very hard and gave her little to eat.

One night, after the holy days of Christmas

had come and gone, Kalyna sat alone before the fire. Outside, a great storm raged. The wind howled down from the icy heights of the ridge, along the gorge of the Czeremoscz River, past the closed doors and windows of the farmhouse and away toward the plains. As Kalyna sat thinking of ways to be rid of Katerina there came a sound, a little sound, like the scratching of fingernails on the wood panels of the wind-shaken door.

Kalyna rose and went to the door, but she was not so silly as to open it straight away. Who knew what might be out on such a wild night? Instead, she said, 'Who is there? Who is there?'

A cold whisper answered above the noise of the storm, 'An old friend. An old friend.'

Kalyna shivered. She was tall and strong and handsome to see yet her heart had long been given to evil things. Now it told her that this was the Ice Woman, she who holds the peaks and uplands in her iron fingers all the long, frozen winter. Kalyna opened the door a crack, and there on the porch stood a thin, old hag with long grey hair and merciless black eyes who shrank from the light and warmth of the fire, far off though it was.

'What do you want? What do you want?' asked Kalyna.

'Passing by, I heard your thoughts. You want to be rid of the child, do you? I need a servant to wash my floors, to comb my hair and carry up the blocks of ice ready to make hail for the winter storms. Send the child to the uplands and you will never see her again!'

Kalyna's cold heart warmed with wickedness. Here

was an answer to the puzzle about what to do to be rid of little Katerina. She said:

> I will send her, I will send her.
> On Saint Eudokia's Day I will send her.
> Keep her in your stronghold
> Where the Sun never comes,
> Where ice hangs blackly
> From the stone walls.

When the Ice Woman heard this she smiled and went quickly away.

Now, when Saint Eudokia's Day comes to the Highlands in the middle of March, it is as though the grace and power of the Saint conquers winter for a while. A mildness breathes across the frozen fields and pastures like a flight of little singing birds. Thick, resinous sap stirs in the hearts of the giant fir trees and they begin to plan the red candles that will burn on every branch. This is not the true Spring when Saint George looses his huge red bull, the mild-eyed one who invisibly warms the world with its breath. It is only the forerunner, the false Spring brought for a little while by the grace of Eudokia, may she be blest! Yet it fitted the plans of the wicked Kalyna.

On Saint Eudokia's Day she said to Katerina, 'The sky is blue, the winds have dropped, Spring has come. Take this basket to the uplands and do not come back till you have filled it with wild raspberries!'

'But mother, the raspberries fruit only in the Autumn,' said Katerina sadly. 'How will I find them in March?'

'Stop arguing and go or it will be the worse for you,' said Kalyna angrily. 'Mind you fill the basket right to the top, too.'

She drove the girl out and away toward the snowfields that reached hungrily down the ridges toward the valleys; toward the high places where the silent streams slept below their cloaks of ice.

Katerina toiled sadly upward through the deep drifts. She knew, as all the people knew, that the blessed Saint George had not yet sounded his trumpet and loosed the Bull who drove the Ice Woman under the Czornohora Ridge to wait in her black caves until the happy Summer had come and gone.

Higher and higher trudged Katerina to the high uplands where the silent trees hung their branches low under their burdens of snow and even the waterfall of the Kizia torrent was stilled in the Old Woman's grasp.

In that solitude of white and black her heart began to fail her and she wept a little though the tears froze on her red cheeks. She remembered to pray to the holy saints: Elias and Nicholas, George and Eudokia. Grace was granted her so that the storms passed her by and blue sky shone above her while the peaks all around were covered with the grey snow clouds.

Without any warning an old woman appeared around a thicket and said, 'Poor little one, what are you doing up here all alone? Night is coming, you will freeze. You had better come home with me and be safe!' She spoke such encouraging words yet all the time she gazed up at the clear blue sky with a look of hatred and she would not come out from the

Many Kinds of Magic

black shadows of the forest. Katerina was young and innocent, she did not know an evil thing when she met one. She was beguiled by the old woman. After all, it was the first kindly word she had heard all Winter. She took her basket and followed up the slope between the black rocks where the old woman led.

When they came to the entrance of a cavern she hesitated, however. Then she felt her wrist seized with steely fingers and she was led helplessly underground. Down and down they went into the heart of the ridge to the home of the Ice Woman. Once there the old woman threw off her disguise and Katerina realized with horror that it was the Ice Woman, the wicked one, who had caught her.

In the time of her captivity that followed Katerina forgot all that was kindly and warm and loving, save for one thing. Under her blouse she wore a little golden crucifix her father had once given her, and though the rest of her body seemed to freeze, yet the holy cross kept her heart from freezing and so she did not become altogether a slave of the wicked one. Though she was made to carry great blocks of ice from the lowest caves up to the heights to make the hail for the storms, though she was forced to comb her cruel mistress's hair with a comb of icicles, though she was compelled to wash the bitterly cold floors and spray the walls with fresh hoar frost, her warm heart saved her from despair.

One day as she toiled upward with a great block of ice she saw the crack of another tunnel leading off from the underground path she followed. The cross around her neck seemed to tug her toward the tiny opening. She let the ice crash to the cold stone and slipped quickly into the cleft. She felt prepared to face any danger, even death itself, to escape from her cruel tormentor. The crevice thinned and narrowed until it was all she could do to force her way past the rough sides, but always she struggled through. At last, far in the distance she caught a glimpse of light. The roof of the tunnel lifted above her, the walls fell back. She found she was able to walk easily upright. Even the floor smoothed out. A puff of warmer air came to greet her. She walked toward the light and came from the tunnel on to the level flagstoned floor of a cavern where a bright flame danced above a cleft in the floor.

She had been in darkness for so long that for a moment the light quite blinded her. Then her eyes warmed to their task, and her heart warmed also, for all around on the benches lining the cavern walls were gaily dressed young men, sleeping as men do after they have worked long and hard then feasted well. Near the flame in a carved stone chair like a throne slept the man who must be their chieftain. He was young with a mop of long, curling black hair and as he slept, he smiled quietly as if dreaming of something that pleased him greatly.

He was dressed like a wealthy mountain farmer in trousers of thick crimson cloth and a rough, embroidered shirt. Over the shirt he wore a sleeveless jerkin of tanned leather richly ornamented with silken embroidery, tassels of scarlet wool and bright brass studs. Over each brawny shoulder went a brass chain, crossing on his breast, to support a very wide, thick leather belt. Through the belt were thrust two

Many Kinds of Magic

pistols, engraved and crusted with gold. On his head he wore the wide-brimmed hat of the mountains, in which were thrust peacock's feathers, and on his feet were high leather boots. On a little stone table close by was a small, wooden pipe. You could see just by looking at it that the tunes it would play would be musical and stirring. Katerina was a little afraid, yet she felt comforted to be with her own people again.

She crept silently closer to the flickering flame and for the first time in many days warmth returned to her frozen body. She knew now where she was! This was the secret cave of Dobosz, the great outlaw and leader of the mountain men who had freed the people from tyranny many years before. She remembered her father and his friends saying that Dobosz was not dead, no matter what the nobility claimed. After freeing the land from slavery he had gone to sleep with his reckless band of young fighters in his secret cave under Czornohora. There they would sleep until the country again groaned under a conqueror's heel. Then they would waken and once more drive out the enemy as they had done so often before. Katerina knew that this was the cave of the heroes, and here they were in holy sleep until they were needed once more. The knowledge warmed her as much as the fire had done. She walked softly across the huge flag-stones to stare at the face of the great Dobosz.

She remembered her father saying, 'He was a terrible foe to our enemies, but to the mountain people he was our father and our brother, and he swore to care for us all.' Thinking of this she sighed, remembering her own plight. If only her father were there to care for her. Turning away, she walked toward the entrance of the cavern, not the cleft through which she had entered but the broad tunnel she was sure must lead to the world outside.

As she went, she passed the doors of many chambers carved in the rock. They were heaped with piles of weapons, the walls were hung with steel axes and swords, and the floors were heaped with gold and jewels. Everything was hushed, as quiet and holy as a church. She slipped along silent as water in a deep channel, the only noise was the soft swish of her leather boots on the clean, stone floor.

When she reached the entrance to the cave she stopped in horror. Waiting for her outside was the Ice Woman! That evil one could not come into the sacred place where the heroes slept, but out on the crags and precipices she still reigned! She was waiting for Katerina, to enslave her again! She was howling like a great wind, angry at losing her servant.

Katerina was appalled. She ran quickly back to the inner cave where the heroes slept. The old woman would never dare invade the resting place of the great Dobosz! Yet Katerina knew that she was trapped here, and that hunger would overcome her soon, for she was starving. The old woman had given her hardly anything to eat and it seemed an eternity since her last meal. She decided that she would stay in this place rather than become a slave again. She was a true daughter of the mountains!

'Better to starve and die among warriors than live a slave,' she thought. Now, that was the watchword of this band of young men. She went timidly to where the little wooden pipe lay on the table. With a quick bow to the sleeping chieftain, she took it and sat beside the eternal flame. She thought that if she played on it a little as her father had taught her then it might drive the hunger from her mind.

She breathed gently into the old, pierced wood and a sweet note came from it. She breathed and fingered slowly and softly and the music began to sing clearly and gently around her. At the sound of the sweet tones there was a tiny glimmer of reflected firelight between the eyelids of the great Dobosz, though Katerina did not notice and the rest of the young men slept on. Then she began to play Dobosz' own song, the song that men still sing today:

> The fir cones are showing red on the uplands,
> Brothers, this year shall we join the robbers?

At the sound of this loved tune the eyes of the sleeper opened wide, and he turned his handsome head to look at her. He studied her quietly while she went on softly playing, unaware of his regard. Presently he stirred and rose gracefully. Hearing the rustle of his garments and the jingling of his ornaments Katerina stopped playing and watched him wide-eyed as he came toward her.

'What is the matter, little daughter? Is the land in danger? Do the nobility need another lesson? Is the Old Emperor stirring? Is Archi-Judas freed? Speak, do not be frightened.'

Katerina remembered her father's words and was comforted. 'He was our father and our brother and he swore to care for us all.' She told him what had happened, quietly explaining to him as if indeed he was her own poor father. He listened in silence until she had ended, then nodded gravely.

'No need to wake my young warriors for this,' he said, nodding toward the sleeping figures who remained unstirring on the benches. 'This is not soldier's work, this is a task for the old saints, the old farmers of the world who plant all seeds and tend all cattle; the tame ones of field and pasture as well as the wild ones of forest and mountainside. You say it is near Spring? Then they will be waiting around their fire for the right day to arrive. Then they will loose the great Bull whose breath frees the water from the Ice Woman's power so it can melt and roar in joy of the great torrents and waterfalls coming down from the highlands to the plains. So we once rode and roared, me and my brothers, when we descended from the hills and broke the powers of the nobles who oppressed our people. Come, little sister, we will find the old saints and they will do what they will do.'

He flung a great white cloak like a wedding garment around his sturdy shoulders and took his steel axe in hand. With his other hand he drew Katerina under the shelter of the cloak and the pair set off by a secret underground way. She was very tired by now, but she went warm and comforted as though it really was her own father who was caring for her. They came from under the earth at last and into a small, clear place among thickets where three old men sat round a great heap of glowing embers, smoking their long-stemmed pipes and talking easily together about things no man could have understood even if he had been as wise as the Rabbi of Ostra himself.

The old saints stopped their talking and puffing as the two came to their fire. Motioning Katerina to be silent, Dobosz left her to warm herself by the embers and whispered with the others. She knew he was telling them her story, and she was content. She felt safe with the old saints. She had prayed to them so often she felt they were friends who would know all about her.

When he had ended his story, Dobosz came back to her and said, 'Farewell, little sister. These old fellows will take care of you now. I must go back to my little nap. Tell the people to love freedom and remember Dobosz whenever they see the red fir-cones catch fire after the hard winter.' She kissed his hand and clung to him. He rested his hand gently on her head for a second, then turned away and vanished. She looked shyly at the old men in their long robes but they did not seem to notice her.

Then one turned his head and said, 'Katerina, we have heard you calling us often and we know your heart. You may go home now. The Ice Woman will not interfere with you, for we will fill this basket with the coals from our living fire to warm your hands as you go down the long, snowy slopes. When you get home, no one will wonder that you have been away so long, for we have taken you back to the day you left to seek raspberries.' He took up a basket and shovelled it full of the glowing embers with his hands so it was heaped to the brim.

Katerina bowed solemnly to all three, but they were once more caught up in their conversation and did not seem to notice. She turned away and started the long journey down the ridge toward home. She turned to wave and bow again just before she rounded the thicket out of sight, and to her surprise both saints and fire had vanished and all was un-trodden snow. Yet the coals glowed in the basket and brought great comfort to her.

When Katerina reached the farm where she knew Kalyna would be waiting her heart almost failed her. Who would believe the story she had to tell? Her father's brother and her other relations would think she was mad if she told them what had happened to her and of Kalyna's harsh treatment. Who would believe the word of a little girl against the story of such a handsome, strong woman as her stepmother? Katerina looked down, thinking that at least the coals would be some sort of evidence of her tale. To her amazement the coals had vanished and the basket was now filled with choice raspberries; glowing and red as the coals had been. She was so hungry that she popped two or three into her mouth before she realized what she was doing. As soon as she swallowed the fruit the virtue in it made her remember that the old saints were with her, and that she must trust them. They were still caring for her, there was no need for fear.

She opened the door and entered, crying, 'Here are your raspberries, mother, just as you needed them! Fine big ones, too! The bushes under Czornohora are loaded with them. I'm only sorry I didn't have another basket to fill as well as this one!'

Kalyna stared unbelievingly at Katerina. She had never expected to see her again.

Katerina put the basket on the table. 'Do taste one, mother, they are sweet as honey,' she said.

Kalyna reached out and took one of the rasp-berries. She chewed thoughtfully on it and swallowed, still staring at Katerina. As soon as she had eaten the fruit the power of the old saints began to work. 'True, true. They are delicious. Mmmmmm! Let me have some more! Oh, yes. I must go and collect some myself. How we'll startle the neighbours, especially the priest's wife! Get my big cloak and the basket for me, daughter; I'm off to the heights to fill it!'

So she went with the basket slung on her back, and as she climbed, the blue sky of Saint Eudokia's Day dwindled to grey above her and over the heights of Czornohora, thunder rumbled and lightning glared.

Kalyna never returned, for as soon as she reached the Ice Woman's domain the old sorceress grabbed her. Ever since she has been forced to work, carrying blocks of ice to the summits to make hailstorms and combing the witch's locks with a rake of icicles.

Katerina grew up and married a fine young farmer with a mop of black curly hair, and their family still keeps alive the memory of Dobosz and the old saints who chain the Ice Woman every Spring; who care for the seed and animals, both wild and tame, of the Czornohora and all the world. They are the ones who free the water so it rushes and roars down the valleys as wild and impetuous as the horsemen of Dobosz.

WEEINGA AND THE WULGURU

Once there was an old magician, a clever fellow, named Tcharapa. He knew a lot about magic but he didn't have much commonsense. He stayed with another old clever man who was dying. Before this old man died, he taught Tcharapa a very strong magic he knew, but he had had too much sense to use it. Tcharapa was vain. He thought he was clever. After the other old man died, Tcharapa went out into the bush by himself and he used that magic. He made a kind of monster man. He carved the arms and legs, the head and body from green timber, and he made shoulders and knees and wrists and elbows from round stones from the riverbed. He tied it all together with string and rubbed it over with red ochre. He painted an awful face on it, then he got his tap-sticks and sang the magic over it. He sang for days and nights, days and nights till his voice got too tired to sing any more. The Thing didn't move, so he gave up in disgust. He thought the song was no good, it wasn't working. He thought he'd better go back to his family.

He picked up his weapons and started to walk through the bush to where his people were camped. There was an awful crashing and crushing sound behind him. He looked round and found that the Thing was following him! It still had its eyes closed but it frightened the white cockatoos and when they screeched it opened its eyes. They glittered like stars.

Tcharapa saw that the Thing wasn't following his tracks, it was watching and listening. That's how it was following him. He ran ahead and hid behind a salmon-gum tree near a deep waterhole. He watched from hiding. The monster walked straight ahead into the water and under the water and kept walking till its head came above the surface on the far side of the lagoon. It just kept on straight ahead then, crashing along through the undergrowth and out of sight. Then Tcharapa was able to go safely home. But the Thing went on living; it was alive now. Its name was Wulguru. After that it only came out at night and its friend was the curlew.

The Wulguru was always looking for children to eat, especially naughty ones who hit the campfire at night to see the sparks fly up, and the ones who went away from their families into the bush and didn't do what they were told. The Wulguru was very strong. Even the old people, who are wisest, couldn't kill the Wulguru, though they could sing songs to drive it away. There was only one little girl who saw the Wulguru and got away. Her name was Weeinga.

Weeinga was very naughty. She used to go off into the bush on her own looking for food without telling anyone where she was going. Her family were always worried about her and warned her all the time but she didn't care. She was a very good tracker and she said she couldn't get lost because all she had to do was to follow her own tracks back to the camp. So she went on being naughty.

One night when everyone was asleep the curlew found Weeinga's tracks at a place where she shouldn't have been. It called its friend the Wulguru and they made a magic together. Weeinga dreamed that her kind grandmother was calling her to get some lovely food. She was still asleep but she got up and walked away from the campfire where she was safe and went into the bush. Then she was dreaming she was finding the food and it was lovely to eat. The Wulguru sneaked up and grabbed her by the wrist. Now she woke up and screamed and screamed, but nobody heard her except the Wulguru and the curlew, and they didn't care!

The Wulguru's eyes shone like green moons, his teeth stuck out of his lips when he grinned as he thought of the fat little girl he had to eat! His skinny fingers held her wrist as he scuttled along like a big spider through the dark and moonlit patches of the hills and gullies of the bush. The curlew went with them for a while, calling and calling like a lost baby, but it got left behind. Weeinga kept on shouting and struggling for a while but you can't get away from a Wulguru. It hangs on like a big octopus, like a scaly python. Weeinga was sorry now that she hadn't listened to the old people, but it was too late for that.

After a while Weeinga knew that being frightened wouldn't help her. She could smell the awful smell of the Wulguru, and feel its sharp nails cutting into the soft skin of her wrist. She pretended to faint so it had to drag her along. She got on the wrong side of trees so it had to stop and untangle her. She tried everything she could think of to slow it down because she knew as soon as they got to its cave it would eat her.

When they got near the stony devil country the sun started to come up and she knew she had slowed him enough. Wulguru's can't stand sunlight, they have to be in the shade in the daytime. It dragged her into a cave on a hillside to wait for nightfall to finish the journey. It got a piece of rope and tied her wrist tightly to its own so when it went to sleep she couldn't get away without waking it up.

When the Wulguru started snoring horribly, Weeinga looked around. There were paintings on the walls of the cave but she didn't look at them because they were men's paintings and women shouldn't see them. But they comforted her because she knew it was her people who had made them. She sat and stared at the floor of the cave while the Wulguru snored like a thunderstorm. Weeinga saw there were little bits of red and yellow ochre mixed in the sand on the cave floor where the men had dropped them, also pieces of white pipe-clay and charcoal. Little bits of paint-stone. They gave her an idea.

She moved carefully so she wouldn't disturb the monster. She took little bits of paint-stone and ground them into powder on a flat stone. She spat on them to wet them. Then, slowly and very carefully she drew a face on the Wulguru's thigh. It was an awful face, the face of the only thing in the world that eats Wulgurus. She was even frightened of it herself when she was finished, it looked so horrible.

Many Kinds of Magic

While it dried she carefully loosened the rope so she could escape from it with a single tug. Then she screamed as loudly as she could and woke the Wulguru.

It stared at her in great anger. 'Why are you screaming?' it shouted. She pointed at the face on its leg. It howled terribly when it saw it. It opened its huge mouth and snapped as hard as it could. It bit right through its leg trying to bite its enemy's head off! Weeinga pulled her arm free, snatched up the leg and ran from the cave. She ran so fast her feet hardly seemed to touch the ground. The monster howled terribly behind her and tried to chase her but it only had one leg now and had to hop like a kangaroo, so it kept falling over.

She had been clever. If she had left the leg it might have been able to stick it on again with magic, but now it couldn't catch her. She ran along the gullies all the hot afternoon, swinging the leg in her hand. The howling of the Wulguru grew fainter and fainter behind her. Her mother and father and her uncles were out looking for her, and when she met them they hurried her off to the safety of the camp.

The wise old people listened to her story. Then they lit a special sort of fire and sang to it. They put the Wulguru's leg on the fire and watched while it spat and frizzled itself to ashes.

When it was gone they called all the children to them and told them to watch out from then on. They must never go alone into the bush without telling someone where they were going. They mustn't hit the fire with sticks at night to see the sparks fly because that might bring the curlew and it would tell the Wulguru where they were. And especially, if they got caught or lost, they must never be frightened but must think very hard so they might get home safely if they could.

(From the Waddaman people of western Arnhem Land)

THE DOONHILL FIDDLER

There was once a fine big strong lump of a lad in Ireland named Michael Kelly and everyone called him Michaeleen Rua, or Little Red Michael because his uncle had the same name and because he had a thick thatch of red curly hair on his head. Michaeleen Rua was not much use at all at gathering kelp or digging peat or ploughing land or tending the cattle; but at dancing and singing and leaping and sporting and kissing young girls there was none to best him in Connacht. Around his hat he wore a green ribbon, and though he was hardly ever at the harvesting or the stone-breaking you could be sure to find him at every wake and wedding and jollification the width of the land.

Michael wanted most in the world to be a fine fiddler as his grandfather had been before him, but no matter how hard he tried or how long he practised the skill would not come to him. He'd take his grandfather's old fiddle out of the case and unwrap it from the faded bit of red silk and he would scrape away, but the noises he made with it was like

137

the cats at Kilkenny Fair fighting the world and each other. It was a great sadness to him and he would be often fiddling when he should have been working at the farming, so he was always poor and yet he made no sort of progression toward being a musician such as he dreamed of being.

One twilight as the long shadows fell across the land he was sitting on the green Hill of Doon with the fiddle on his lap and himself in tears for he'd been trying to get the swing of a reel out of the instrument and had failed entirely. He heard a small voice saying, 'Little Red Michael, why are you weeping?'

He looked up and saw it was a short, wide woman in a hooded cloak, and if he had been standing the top of her head would only have come up level with the buckle of his belt.

'It's meself would prefer to be a fiddler and not an old agricultural labourer but for the life of me I can't get reel, jig nor lament to ring from the wood the way it should,' he confessed. 'Also I've been sitting here all afternoon and not a drop to drink has passed me lips and I'm tolerably dry in the throat.'

The woman said, 'Well now, I've been sent to find a shinty player, not a fiddle player, and I fear you're no use to me at all.'

'A shinty player, is it?' said Michael, rising to his feet. 'You have come to the right man after all. Put a stick in my hands and devil the man in Connacht whose shins would be safe from me and me in flight after the ball. Try me, that's all!'

'Them's bold words, me bold man,' said the woman. 'Well, it's worth trying, I suppose. Follow me, now and I'll bring you where you might be able to

Many Kinds of Magic

end the thirst that's troubling you.'

'Lead away. I'm your man for a bit of sport!' said Michael, folding the fiddle away in its case.

They went down the hill to a deep narrow cleft with rocky walls and trees growing both sides so their branches met overhead. The little woman spoke a word or three he didn't understand and then Michael saw an open door in the side of the hill, and through the door a great room where many little people were dancing and moving to the sound of pipes and fiddles. There were all kinds of dainties to eat and drink laid out on trestles, and the couple who led the dance were taller than the others and their clothes shone with gold and pretty gemstones, and they wore gold crowns on their heads.

Michael knew where he had been taken then. This was the fairy court of Finvara and Nuala, high King and Queen of the little people of Connacht, the Shee. When the fiddlers and pipers had finished scraping and puffing the royal pair came to where Michael was standing beside his guide.

'Is it yourself, Michaeleen Kelly?' asked the King. 'Many's the time I've heard you tormenting the poor instrument you carry with you in the hopes of becoming a musician. A sorrier sound I've never heard!'

'It's meself, your Majesty,' said Michaeleen Rua.

'Is there a thirst to you?' asked the Queen kindly.

'I could stand to take a drink,' admitted Michael.

She took him by the hand and led him to where the musicians were burying their noses in the froth of the ale and the ruby of the wine, and ordered that he be given drink. When he was finished and had wiped his hand across the mouth like anyone would, the King said, 'Every year the Fairy Host of Connacht go to play at the shinty with the Host of Munster, King Nephin's people. Both sides take a mortal man with them to see fair play. Will you come?'

'Indeed, I'm your man!' said Michael. 'I'll go with you and come back with you and devil a bit of unfairness will I allow.'

'My fine man!' said the King happily. 'Before we go, will you take your fiddle and join my gleemen and help with the next dance?'

'Your Majesty's a brave fellow to ask me for music, but I'll do what I can,' said Michael. He took the fiddle from its case and unrolled it from the silk, then took his stand beside the fairy men. The King smiled and touched first the fiddle, then the bow, then last of all he touched Michael on the elbow with his fingertip. Then he took the Queen's hand and led her out to the circle of dancers.

The little fiddlers and pipers struck up 'The Sands Of Breffni' so well that Michael was ashamed to begin with them, so featly did they play. To his surprise his elbow crooked of itself, the fiddle flew under his chin and he found he was playing as quick and neat and tuneful as any there. He was happier than he had ever been in his life before as the swift notes danced and leapt and poured from the instrument and the dancers swayed and rose and fell like the waters of the sea itself under the spell of the music. When the dance was done he shouted aloud with joy and could have gone on playing all night.

The King raised his arms for silence, then said loudly, 'All of you to Moytura Waste or the men of

Many Kinds of Magic

the Host of Nephin will be on the field before us and jeer at us for laggards!' Then rose a shouting and rushing and cheering such as you never heard before and in a way he couldn't rightly understand Michael found himself astride a broom besom and away through the air with the high-riding Host. It seemed no time at all till they came to Moytura under Slieve Belgadaun and found the Host of Nephin's Rath, the Munster Shee, assembled and with them a mortal man of their own choosing to be their judge and see fair play for their side also.

The ball was soon thrown in and the little people began smiting at it with their hurley sticks. Back and forth,. from side to side, went the fortunes of the game until Michaeleen saw a Munster fairy playing unfair. He shouted aloud about this but his judgement was questioned by the mortal who had come from Munster. A great ugly black-browed fellow he was with a face like the water-bull and bowed legs like the rib-bones of a whale. He was such a disputatious man that he gave over all kind of genteel behaviour and began poking Michael in the chest which no loyal man from Connacht could abide from such a gangrel as he. Michael put down his fiddle and put up his fists and soon they were at it, boots, thumbs and all. Their wrestling and striking and gripping and falling about made the soft places hard and the hard places soft and the water to be wrung from the grey stones and the sparks to fly from the red stones.

In a while Michael got in a good lick or two and the black-browed fellow cried for mercy, the way of him having five ribs sadly bent and his left leg twisted so it wouldn't bear him upright and he kept falling to one side. Michael looked round and found the shinty had stopped and the battle begun and nearly over; the Host of Munster flying off like a swarm of bees and the Connacht Shee holding the ground, so he let the beaten fellow get to his feet and limp away after them.

Then there rose a great sound of cheering and exultation from the Host of Finvara and all took horse and broom back in a riotous procession to the Hill of Doon, for they had the victory for that year. Healths went round in honey mead and good ale and red wine and Michael's name was toasted with the rest of the heroes. When the feasting was over and all was quiet again the little old woman came to Michael and said, 'It's time for you leave now. Finvara has decreed you can keep the skill of fiddle and bow he granted you because of the fine way you put down that ugly black-browed mortal Them Ones brought with them to the shinty.'

She led him out the narrow, tree-grown place to the hillside where he was astonished to find no time at all had gone by. The twilight lay quiet and hushed upon the long green slopes and the grazing cattle were still in the same places where they had been feeding before.

'Be here tomorrow evening at the same time,' said the little old woman. 'Himself has another task for you on the morrow now he has seen what a fine resolute warlike fellow you are.'

'I'll be here when you come,' said Michaeleen Rua. When she had vanished he took out the fiddle and tried a few notes on it. To his joy he had kept the skill he was given and the sound of bow on strings drew the late lark from the sky and even the nightingale hushed her song to listen. Content, he put the instrument away and went off downhill to his cottage where he slept sound from the contentment of his music and also from all the ale he had drunk.

You can be sure he was early on the hillside next evening with his fiddle and his new skill. He seated himself on a green bank and began to play 'The Londonderry Air' with such sweetness and sorrow he began to weep from the joy of feeling so sad and being so skilful. Presently he saw the fairy woman standing beside him, though he could not begin to understand how she came there.

'Come along, Red Michael,' she said. 'Himself is waiting.'

He sprang from the ground, dashed the tears from his cheeks, and followed her steps through the glen and under the slopes into the fairy stronghold. Sure enough, Finvara was waiting for him, alone save for his Druid that stood cloaked behind him, and there was no dancing or drinking going on at this time.

'Hail, King,' said Michael.

'Good evening to you, Michaeleen,' said the King. 'Last night you showed us you were a brave fellow and a good man of your hands, being able to best that black-browed man of Munster. Now, me Druid Conan here thinks you might be able to rid me of a more dangerous pest than him; one that's forever breaking the peace of the realm, besides eating maidens and breathing poison on the crops – that way the barley gets tainted and makes the October ale taste like croton oil.'

'What like of a thing is it that's troubling you?' asked Michael.

'It's a Sinech, a water-monster; a kind of great slippery worm with a mouthful of poison all cold and green and deadly that would blacken the robes of the Banshee. It's long as a shinty field and thin as a serpent and has a temper worse than Gentle Annis or the Brown Bull itself.'

Michael thought about it, for though he wasn't afraid of any man who trod the sod, yet this was something different.

'I doubt I'd be able to handle it with me bare hands, your Highness,' he said, being honest. 'Maybe the good Conan might advise me on how I'd better be going about it.'

The Druid stepped forward. 'It's the wise man you are to be asking the help of them that can give it,' he said grandly. 'I'll tell you what I think, boy. In the King's treasure house is a sword of great charm, being fatal to anything of a magic nature. Now, none of the Shee can handle or swing the Sword of Nuada, but you being a mortal, then the charm won't harm you. You could take it in your two hands and do great killings and executions with it. It is fatal to any Thing of Fairy that it wounds. Now, what do you think about being lent that to take up against this Sinech?'

'It sounds like a good thing to take along on such a journey,' said Michael cautiously. 'Tell me, if you were after lending me the Sword of Nuada, where might I find the Sinech? Would I have to go alone? I'm not in favour of a serpent that steals maidens, that's a great waste; besides, spoiling the flavour of good ale is a thing that doesn't bear thinking on.'

'Where is it? Why, it's at Lough Gara just now, frightening the otters there so they're sad at not being able to make their teeth meet in a salmon without looking over their shoulders all the time.'

Michael looked at Finvara, but the King kept his council and Conan also fell silent. At last Michael said, 'It sounds a sport to beat the running of horses and the following of hounds. Maybe I'll go there and take a look at this old Sinech, if someone will come with me for company.'

'No sooner said than done,' said Conan, taking a long, carefully wrapped bundle from under his black cloak and offering it to Michael. 'Would you mind carrying the sword, meantime, because the magic of it keeps gnawing at me even through the spells and wrappings I've put round it; and it would be better so, for then I can concentrate on the spells I'll be making to take us there. Here, take the sword.'

Michael took the bundle and a heavy one it was, dragging at his arms. He left the fiddle with the little old fairy woman so it mightn't be bruised in the battle, hefted the bundled sword and waited. Conan turned three times muttering, seized him by the shoulder and in a little time, he wasn't sure how, they were standing on the bleak shores of a stretch of grey water under a grey sky with the wavelets beating on the gravel at their feet and the silk of the bog cotton blowing in the wind around them.

The wind was cold and the sword was heavy. Michael began to have doubts. How was he to smite and gash and slice the Sinech with a weapon that was half as heavy as himself?

'That old Sinech will be sitting down in his coils in the black dregs of the fathomless water chewing some poor girleen he's captured,' said Conan. 'Maybe you'll have to call him in a captivating way so he'll rise toward you.' Saying which he walked a long way back from the water's brink and stood as though he might be ready to run for it.

'Will you not stand with me?' asked Michael nervously.

'It's giving you plenty of room for your great sword-arm I am,' explained the Druid, and he came no nearer.

Michael began to unwrap the blade. 'Time I was starting and so getting closer to finishing,' he said. The sword was of dull-grey grainy-looking steel, rough-cast but with an edge to it that would shave the hair off the belly of a bee. It had a two-handed grip behind a steel hilt, and as Michael took it from the last of the wrappings it began to glow with a dull light and became as light to his hands as a rush or a reed of the water.

'It's the magic in it working, you see,' explained Conan, edging further away. 'Surely there's a power in it gives me a hangover worse than three nights drinking October ale.'

Michael walked to the edge of the water and stirred it with the point of the sword. 'Come out, old Sinech, come out and meet your admirer that wants to put a question to you!' he shouted for he felt more cheerful now he had seen and hefted his weapon. Nothing happened for a while and he was about to shout again when a little whirlpool appeared on the surface of the grey water out in the deeps and the wind blew more shrill and cold, stirring the rushes and the reeds. From under the water came a big head with great eyes and chewing jaws on the top of a long scaly neck with a mane on it like a stallion. It swallowed and regarded Michael balefully, and him standing there all soft-looking on the bank with the sword half-hidden behind his leg.

'What would such as you be wanting from such as me?' it asked proud and haughty.

'You took your time coming up to meet and see me,' remarked Michael as bravely as he was able after seeing such a dreadful thing.

'I was eating a maiden,' said the Sinech. 'Me mother told me it was bad manners to be talking with your mouth full. I asked you, what do you want? Is it something to do with that old black crow that's standing back there in the distance so far I can't reach him with me neck to champ him in me chops, not that anyone would want to meet their teeth in such a pitiful strawneen.'

Conan roared with anger at this description of himself, but Michael noticed he came no closer for all that.

'What was I wanting? I'll tell you what I was wanting. It was to know how such a slippery, ugly, horse-faced, slimy-eyed wastrel of a thing as you escaped when the blessed Patrick chased your relatives from the green island, seed, breed and generation.'

'Not that it's any of your two-legged, smellful, potato-eating business,' said the Sinech nastily, 'but I happened to be on a visit to me relatives in Lough Ness in the Pictish lands at the time and missed the ban of that interfering old saint and was able to come back to me own place in me own good time, here to Lough Gara of the deep water. Now, there's your answer for you and much good may it do you.'

'I've heard of your relatives and a nasty lot they are; but there's not a one of them uglier nor of a worse smell or aspect than your moulting, mouldy, bad-distributed self, may the Devil run away with you and use you for a poker,' said Michael, who was warming a little after what the Sinech had called him. 'Wasn't it yourself that had the mother Finn McCool caught and made into a great eel pie for himself and the Fianna, and they all suffering a great bellyache after eating her and spitting out her bones? Wasn't it yourself that tried to catch the Salmon of Lough Dearg and failed dismal, and all about laughing at you?'

The Sinech stopped submerging and roared, 'I did not!'

'You did so! The world knows it! Didn't me grand-father's own cousin tell him so, and he told me father, and me father told me!'

The huge creature roared again and this time ripples showed behind its neck. It raised its head so far out of the water at the end of its long neck that no doubt it could hear Mass being said in Heaven. It sped so furiously across the lough and its speed was so great that its belly ran upon the gravel of the shore and stranded its front end, the while swinging its wide jaws around after Michael, trying to breathe poison on him and chew him as well so it got muddled in its thought trying to do both at once.

Michael meantime was busy as a crubeen-seller at

Many Kinds of Magic

the Galway Races. He leapt to the front, the back and to both sides all at the same time and the sword went 'Swissssssssh! Swisssxsssssh!' around his head like the sails of a windmill. It wasn't much skill he had but he showed great energy. In a while the Sinech thrust out its head when it should have been withdrawing it and the sword went 'Sniiiiiiiiick!' and the head went rolling along the margin of the lake like a football and trying to get back to the spouting neck so it could join itself back by magic, the way Sinechs could do.

But Michael was too quick and he smote again and again till the head and the eyes and the tangled bit of mane was cut into bits like the making of a sausage, and all magic has to fail against workmanship like that.

'Hurrooo for the men of Connacht!' shouted Michael, leaping up and down for joy and waving the sword around dangerously. He was near chopping off his own head in his joy and exultation and as it was, Conan had two narrow squeaks before he regained a safe distance.

'Well done, me fine hero,' said the Druid, coming forward as the sword stopped swinging. 'Now, if you wouldn't mind just wrapping up the blade in the insulation, so to speak, I'll take charge of it against.'

'You're frightened by it, aren't you?' demanded Michael.

'With someone like you making a whirraroo like that, who wouldn't be?' demanded the Druid bitterly.

'That's not what I mean, old Druid,' said Michael. 'It's the magic that's in it that's got you worried more

than me swishing it in me pardonable excitement.
Isn't it?'

'I'll admit it has powers of its own. Now, be a good
lad and hand it back in its wrappings before I see
me way clear to turning you into a toad or something unpleasant.'

'I think that with this in me hand and the power
that's in it you couldn't turn me into anything at all.'

Conan smiled gently. 'That might be true or it
might not, but remember, to stay safe you'd have to
hold it all the time, and that could be awkward in
the nights when you'd have to take it to your bed.
So sharp it is, and you with maybe a drink or five
in you, you'd easy roll on it in the night and wake
with some fingers or toes missing from you, or maybe
even something else you'd miss more.'

Michael picked up the wrappings and swathed the
sword in them and handed it back to Conan. 'Here's
your old sword then,' he grumbled. 'I was just
thinking what a fine cutter it would have made for
the turf-bog, that's all.'

'Save us all,' muttered Conan. 'The Sword of
Nuada to cut the peat for him, indeed!'

'Ah, forget it and let's be getting back. Me throat
is dry as a limeburner's boot,' said Michael.

Soon they were back in the fairy stronghold of
Finvara and great was the row of cheering and
shouting and singing and music when Conan
gave the news that the Sinech was passed away.
In the celebration that followed, none drank more
or danced longer or played more tunefully than
Michael himself. When the party was over and
most were sleeping Finvara himself led Michaeleen

Rua to the door of the rath.

'We're grateful to you for all you've done for us,' he said.

'Maybe you'd like to give me some small memento, then,' said Michael slowly, looking sideways at Conan.

'You've got the power of music, and that's no small thing,' said the Druid. He looked as though he was still remembering the difficulty he'd had with the lad over the sword.

'I was just coming to that,' said Finvara. He reached into the bosom of his robe and took out a small flask just the size might fit into the coat pocket of a fiddler. 'Let you be wetting your lips with this.'

Michaeleen took a draw at the neck, and tears came to his eyes. 'It's surely a drink with a great power and authority to it,' he said when he could breathe easy once more.

'I'm giving it to you to keep me in memory,' said the Lord of the Shee. 'If you raise it toward Knock Math every time you drink in a toast to us all, then it has the virtue that it will never run dry.'

'Then it's the right kind of a flask for a fiddler to have on his hip,' said Michael happily. 'My grateful thanks to your Majesty. Maybe I'd better be going now.'

'Wait you one moment,' said Finvara kindly. 'I have the good advice for you, a kindly word that might bring you more joy in the end than the music or the flask. Remember this, Michael Kelly, all the days of your life. No men and no nation can ever be beat while the happy noise of their singing and dancing go on among the people. You will become a wandering man of the roads with your fiddle and your flask, and you'll maybe put the strong hand at the throat of them you find oppressing the common people now and then; but you will make new songs and new tunes and new tales, and those will go on long after men have forgotten your name. That is the last and best of my blessings on you for the services you have done me. Now, may you find the good road before you and all harm behind you and a light heart always to help you lift your tired boots. Farewell, Little Michael Kelly.'

At that he dropped his hand that had been raised in a blessing and the door to the fairy stronghold closed. Once more Michael found himself on the green hillside, and when he looked round, no time at all seemed to have passed. For a moment he was sad that he would never see the fair folk again, then he took a small suck at his flask, struck up 'The Star Of The County Down' on his strings and went off on the long journey that lay ahead of him.

That happened long ago but his spirit is still on the long roads and the truth was with Finvara, for the music and the songs do go on.

ABOGAN IS A GNOME, THIRD CLASS

Once upon a time there was an old gold-miner named Jake (all this happened a long time ago). He had a sulphur-crested cockatoo about thirty years old which lived on a perch outside his hut in the wild bush mountains.

Except for the parrot, which didn't have a name, Jake lived by himself. He spent a lot of time digging holes looking for gold, but he never seemed to find very much; just enough to let him buy some corned beef and a bag of flour and some tea and sugar now and then.

Then he'd go back to the hills to try to find some more gold. It was very frustrating for him. Every now and then he would go and borrow a few cobs of corn to feed the parrot, but that was all he gave it to eat.

The parrot was pretty stupid, even though it was old and experienced. It never learned to say very much. Sometimes it would yell, 'Hands up!' and sometimes it would whisper, 'Where's the gold? Where's the gold? It must be here somewhere!' That was all it ever said. Jake didn't like it very much, but there it was and so he kept on looking after it.

One morning the cockatoo managed to get its leg out of the ring on the end of its chain. It was free. It wasn't a bit grateful for the corn, or loyal to its master. It just flew off into the hills and joined a mob of wild white cockatoos that lived there.

It taught all the other birds to whisper, 'Where's the gold?' and Jake got sick and tired of hearing little voices all round him, asking where the gold was. He was finding hardly any, no matter how many holes he dug. He used to throw stones at every white cockatoo he saw. Sometimes they would say, 'Where's the gold?' then '*Ouch!*' as a stone hit them in the feathers.

One day about dinner time, Jake cracked upon a big rock to see if there was any gold inside. As the stone cracked and fell apart, a Bogan stepped out and stretched itself. The Bogan looked like a little man about forty centimetres high, dressed in big boots, blue trousers and a flannel shirt with no sleeves, and it had a lot of hair and a huge beard. It was very dirty, but it didn't seem to care about that. Actually it was a kind of fairy, in a way, but it hadn't been behaving very well, so the boss Bogan had shut it up in the rock for a few thousand years. That was why it was stretching; it was cramped from being still for so long.

Jake was surprised, just the same as you might have been.

'What in the world are you?' he asked. He'd never seen an ugly, dirty little man like that before.

The Bogan looked at him and scowled. 'I'm a Bogan,' he said. 'Not that it's any of your business, but since it was you that let me out, I suppose I'd

Many Kinds of Magic

better be a bit polite. I was starting to get bored in there.'

'What's a Bogan?' asked Jake.

The little creature frowned, and said thoughtfully, 'Well, you might say that it's a sort of fairy, but that's not the half of it. There's fairies, and Good Fairies, and then there's Bogans.'

The miner thought about it for a while. Then he said, 'If you're a sort of fairy, and I let you out, then I reckon you ought to give me some sort of reward.' And he scratched the side of his neck with the point of his pick.

'Hands up!' yelled fifty cockatoos that had got in a big gum tree close by and were listening in like a lot of stickybeaks.

'Reward?' said the Bogan. 'All everyone thinks about these days is rewards! People used to be happy once just with the good feeling they got from being helpful. Now all they think of is rewards! Ah, well, I suppose I could grant you one wish, as long as you're not too greedy.' And it waved its hand around to chase the flies out of its eyes and ears.

'I thought you blokes were supposed to give us three wishes,' said Jake. This was the only time he'd ever met a fairy, and he thought he'd better make the most of it.

'Three! You greedy old cuss!' said the Bogan. 'Tell you what. We'll split the difference. I'll give you two wishes. Only princes or the sons of poor widows get three.'

About then the fifty cockatoos in the tree whispered, 'Where's the gold? Where's the gold? It must be here somewhere!'

'Gold? Is that what you're interested in?' asked the Bogan.

Jake nodded, but he didn't say anything. He'd read stories about how you had to be careful what you said to fairies or you wasted your wishes, and he didn't want to do that.

'You have to ask for it. Out loud,' said the Bogan angrily.

'All right, all right! I was just going to. I wish – I wish you would tell me where I can find enough gold near here to get me enough money to last me for the rest of my life!'

'Will you listen to him?' said the Bogan in disgust to the cockatoos. 'He seems to think I'm one of those Djinns that go round piling gold up, or something. *Those* are fairies with a higher education, not ordinary blokes like me. I'm only a sort of gnome, third-class. I don't know all *that* much.'

He turned to Jake. 'Now listen! I'll only say it once. If you go up along the next ridge to near the top, you'll find a big tree that's been struck by lightning. Look a bit downhill. There's a bit of gold there, though I don't know if it's enough to last you the rest of your life. There's a fair bit, though!'

Jake frowned. 'Can I save up my other wish till I see how much is there?'

'No, you can't!' said the Bogan. 'I've got more to do than stand around here, getting crawled on by flies, waiting for you to make up your mind. Hurry up!'

Jake stood there quietly for a minute, thinking as fast as he could, which wasn't really very fast. About a thousand more white cockatoos came flying in to see what their fifty mates were looking at so hard. They filled the tops of about ten trees.

Some of them hung upside down and looked backwards over their shoulders because they thought they could see more that way. Some of them raised up their yellow crests and yelled at one another in cockatoo. They were all discussing what was going on in their own language.

Then the stupid cockatoo that had escaped from Jake started to yell, 'Hands up! Hands up!'

All the other cockatoos thought that was a good idea, so they started yelling, 'Hands up!' too. Not that they raised their hands, or rather, their feet; or they would have fallen from the trees! Their screeching and yelling rose above all the other noises, and the Bogan forgot about the flies for a minute or two.

The old miner was furious. 'Shut up, the lot of you,' he screamed back at them.

The cockatoos thought it was a game. 'Hands up!' they shouted like a mob of bushrangers. Some of them started to yell, 'Where's the gold?' too.

'I'm trying to think!' yelled the miner.

'Hurry up, you old bandicoot!' yelled the Bogan.

'Hands up! It must be here somewhere!' yelled the cockatoos.

'Oh, you lot of yeller-headed, milky-faced twits; I wish you were all in Darwin!' yelled Jake, completely doing his temper.

Suddenly everything was still. There wasn't a thing to be heard except for the nasty chuckling of the Bogan as it slipped away downhill towards the dry gully. It was going off to do something wicked that it had thought up while it was trapped in the rock.

Well, Jake was left alone. He found a fair-sized lump of gold where the Bogan had told him. He took it down to Melbourne and got a lot of money for it; but the Melbourne Cup was on just then, and he lost all the money backing racehorses that didn't run very fast.

He didn't care much, though; he just went back to digging for little bits of gold again to pay for his food.

The cockatoos are still up around Darwin. If you ever go up there, and listen very carefully, you might hear them calling. 'Where's the gold? Hands up! Milky-faced twits!' they say. Then they all laugh like mad.

I don't know what happened to the Bogan. I'd keep my eyes open if I were you, though. You never know what it was going to do when it went off like that, and it just might have been going in your direction.

Y OUNG-MAN WHO TRAVELLED

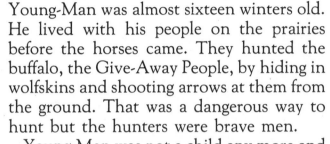

Young-Man was almost sixteen winters old. He lived with his people on the prairies before the horses came. They hunted the buffalo, the Give-Away People, by hiding in wolfskins and shooting arrows at them from the ground. That was a dangerous way to hunt but the hunters were brave men.

Young-Man was not a child any more and did not want to play children's games. Sometimes he helped look after the small ones when they went to the river or some other place where there might be danger but mostly he sat with his friends and they didn't do anything much. He was unhappy a lot of the time. He was bored with his family, bored with the world. He took to walking alone, going away from the village and off towards the mountains. Sometimes he stayed away all night and only came home when he was hungry. His father and mother were patient with him but his sister thought he was silly and often said so.

One day his grandfather said to him, 'You are looking for something, aren't you? What are you looking for?'

159

'I don't know,' said Young-Man. 'Things were all right when I was a Little-Boy but now I am a Young-Man I wonder what life is all about. Do you know what life is all about, grandfather?'

'For me, life is about the ceremonies and the care of the people, and advising the men where to hunt, also helping those who need help. I can see that these things might seem unimportant to a young-man like you but that's the way of it.'

Young-Man's two uncles were listening. They laughed and said, 'We know what's the matter. You are trying to find out what you want to be. Maybe you will be a hunter like we are, to feed the people. Maybe you will be a doctor like grandfather to heal the people. Maybe you will be a crazy man, a care-for-nothing man, a fighter to protect the people from enemies!'

They looked at Young-Man but he shook his head savagely and shouted, 'I don't want to be any of those things! I don't want to! I don't want to! They are all boring!'

Both his uncles laughed at him then, but his grand-father didn't laugh. He said, 'Maybe I can send you to find what you are looking for but you will have to go there by yourself and come back by yourself.'

'What do you mean, grandfather?' asked Young-Man. He wasn't much pleased but at least it didn't sound boring.

'You will have to be a hunter and go on a hunt for what you're looking for, that's what. Oh, we grandfathers know the rules, that's what we're here for! Are you brave? Are you strong? Are you sure you want to do this? It will be hard to begin and harder to finish!'

'Of course I'm sure,' said Young-Man angrily. His uncles laughed again but this time they were not laughing at him, they were laughing admiringly.

'Well, if you are sure, then here's what we'll do,' said grandfather. 'You begin by not eating anything. Tomorrow morning we'll make a sweat-bath and we'll have a ceremony while you are having the sweat-bath. Then you must go the top of the mountain and stay there three days. There will be a hole there, your uncles will dig that for you. You must stay in the hole and think about what you are hunting for. You might ask for Someone to help you, that's always a good idea. You never know, Somebody might get to feeling sorry for you and offer to help you hunt.'

'That's a good idea, *we* both did this when we were Young-Men' said his uncles. 'We'll dig the hole for you, don't worry. You listen to grandfather, he knows what he's talking about! You can't have any clothes, you know, that's part of this hunt. Only grandmother will give you a robe to wear at night while you're up there. Now we're off to dig the hole, we'll see you tomorrow!'

They ran off toward the mountain as fast as they could run, laughing together with happiness. Their feet went swishswishswish in the sweet prairie grass and their laughter died away as they ran, 'HAHAHAHAHahahahah . . . ha . . .'

Next morning Young-Man went to the sweat-bath and sat naked inside while grandfather poured cold water on the red-hot stones to make steam. So much steam came and it was so hot that Young-Man was sorry he had agreed. Then grandfather gave him a red-stone pipe and wrapped him in grandmother's beautiful robe and they went off up and up to the mountain where the hole was ready.

'Get in the hole now. You must sit down. Here is a little bowl of water, be careful with it, it has to last you for three days. Here is the pipe, you must hold it this way when you are asking for advice. Now we are going away. You may wrap yourself in the robe at night but you mustn't wear it during the day.'

Young-Man felt rather silly. He said, 'But what must I do? Three days! I thought this was going to be a hunt. Three days! I had no supper last night and I'm hungry already. Three days!'

'Oh, three days, that's nothing,' said grandfather. 'I did this, so did your father, so did your uncles. You don't want to worry. Just think about what you want to be, and what you're hunting for. If anything happens, or if anyone comes, remember what it is so you can tell me all about it when I come for you.'

'Maybe I might find what I'm looking for without doing all this. Then I could have something to eat.'

'Look, do you want to go around all your life complaining and grumbling? You'll be a Nothing-Man, that's what you'll be! No, you stay here. I'm going away now. Goodbye, goodbye. Keep asking for help.'

Grandfather went away downhill leaving him alone. He could hear grandfather's feet going swish-rattleswishrattlerattle through the grass and over the stones on the steep mountain side. Young-Man was left alone.

All he could think about for a long time was his hunger and how empty he felt. He was thirsty, too, but he didn't have a drink of water because he only

Many Kinds of Magic

had a little and there were three days to go. He folded the beautiful robe neatly and laid it on a stone beside the hole. The grass-clumps swayed in the cool breeze. He could see them clearly because when he was sitting in the hole his head was just level with the top of the ground. Little crumbs of dirt rolled down the sides of the pit when he brushed against them.

Nothing happened.

Young-Man got bored. He sang some songs he knew about the buffalo, the Give-Away People. The sun got higher. It shone down on him in his hole from high overhead.

Nothing happened.

'All right, you people! Who will come and talk to me?' he yelled suddenly. Nobody answered. Nobody came. The sun shone, the wind talked softly to the grass-clumps, the grass danced, bowing to the wind.

Nothing happened.

Nothing . . .? Suddenly Young-Man saw a tiny head peering short-sightedly at him from the bottom of a tussock. It was Prairie-Mouse.

'Hello, Person,' said Young-Man politely. We have met each other before you know. We met often when I was a Small-Boy.'

'I remember, I know,' squeaked Mouse. 'You chased me all over the plains. You thought it was fun to frighten me and make me run. You laughed when I was afraid. You were unkind to me.'

'You looked so funny when you ran!' explained Young-Man, smiling at the memory. 'I liked to see you bounce and skip. Now, maybe you had better go away, I am having a big ceremony and have called for someone to help me. It's sure to be someone grand

and important, so you just hop away.'

Mouse grinned at him. 'Maybe no one will bother to come.'

'Of course they will! Don't you understand? This is *very important*. I am hunting to find out what I'm looking for.'

'It sounds pretty crazy to me. Maybe it's important to you, but I don't think anybody else would think so.'

'My grandfather does! So do my uncles! Why did they send me up here otherwise?'

'*I don't know*! Maybe they got tired of you moaning and glooming and mooning round the camp and thought you'd be better off up here for a few days!'

'You nasty little person!' shouted Young-Man. 'I'll chase you through the tussocks again for saying that!'

'I don't think you will,' said Mouse. 'I don't think you can get out of that hole. Why don't you get out of the hole?'

Sure enough, when Young-Man tried to get out of the hole to chase Mouse, he couldn't!

'I'll just go away now. You are pretty boring anyway. Maybe I'll come back tomorrow and see how you are getting on.' He vanished into the grass and though Young-Man called and called him he wouldn't come back.

He shouted and raged but nothing happened. He tried to get out of the hole, but nothing happened. He seemed to be fixed to the ground. He could turn his head from side to side, he could lift his arms as high as the top of the hole but that was all. He was hungry, he was getting chilled as the sun sank and he was furious. When he tired of shouting at the empty sky and the brown grass and rocks and earth his anger turned to sorrow for himself and he cried and cried real tears that flowed down his cheeks and chest. The sun was level with the western peaks when he stopped crying and simply sat and watched and listened and also stopped feeling sorry for himself. 'After all, it was *me* who decided to come here and do this, so it is *me* who is to blame,' he thought.

As he thought that, shivering with cold, he found he could raise one arm enough to reach out of the hole and pick up the robe his grandmother had made for him. He was grateful for it; it clasped him warmly and he began to feel more cheerful. The Sky-People twinkled at him from the heavens and the little creatures who skip from tussock to tussock began their nightly round of living close by his ears and eyes. Sunk in the ground as he was, this was the first time he had had a proper chance to study them. After a time he raised his eyes to where Evening Star shone and thought to himself, 'There you are in the west, Evening Star Person. Welcome, welcome. I am not doing anything bad, I am just resting here. All you little skippers and tussock-whiskers, do not be afraid of me. I am a good person. Thank you, earth and rocks and grasses for being around me. Please look after me while I rest here. I do not mean any harm, I will just stay in my hole. I can't get out, anyway. Goodnight, mountains and red sunset, care for me while I am sleeping. Goodnight, goodnight all!'

Young-Man huddled under the warm robe but found he could not sleep. A big old Coyote came and sat on a rock not far away and began to howl. At last Young-Man said politely, 'Please, grandfather

Coyote, wouldn't you like to go further away to do your howling?'

'What's this? What's this? A Young-Man, isn't it? Ha ha ha, buried in a hole, too! Are you trying to hunt me? Will you chase me? Anyway, I'm singing, not howling. *You* weren't well brought up, to insult me like that. Howling, indeed! Let me sing again for you, so you can really enjoy yourself. Awoooo. Ahwoooooooo. Ahhhhhwwoooooooooo!'

'*That* doesn't sound like sweet singing to me,' grumbled Young-Man.

'Something wrong with your ears?' asked Coyote. 'Oh, you need to learn how to listen. There's only one place to learn that! The North. Right, off you go to the North!'

'How can I go anywhere. I can't get out of this hole! I'm stuck.'

'Try,' said Coyote, coming nearer. 'You aren't trying hard enough!'

'*I am! I am! Don't tell me I'm not trying!*' shouted Young-Man.

'Ah, such a lazy Young-Man. Not really trying at all,' said Coyote, coming even nearer. Young-Man was so furious that he nearly burst himself trying to reach the person who was teasing him. Suddenly there was a noise like a thong snapping – *thwok* – and he was free.

'Now I'll get you, now I'll teach you to laugh at me!'

But Coyote was already running off as hard as he could go toward the North. Young-Man ran after him. They ran and ran for hours. Every time Young-Man slowed Coyote would wait for him saying, 'Are you weak? Are you failing? Should I carry you for

Many Kinds of Magic

a time?' Then Young-Man would get mad and speed up again.

At length they came to a high ridge of white stone, so long that it reached from horizon to horizon, blocking their way. Coyote ran up the steep slope – flickflickflickflick – easy. Young-Man scrambled after him – strain – puff – strain – puffpuff. Coyote waited for him on a flat rock just below the summit of the ridge. Just as Young-Man came to where he could reach out in triumph and grab hold of Coyote's bushy tail a huge head came looming into sight over the ridge-top and a booming voice said, 'Hullo, Old Coyote. Welcome, welcome, Old Man. What is the trouble here? Is this Young-Man making war on you? Is he a crazy man, a warrior man, a bravery enemy-way man? Shall I protect you from him? Shall I stomp him with my hoofs and pierce him with my horns?'

It was Old Buffalo Bull, most powerful Chief of the Give-Away People! He was enormous, with curly hair on his forehead and horns as straight and long as lodge-pole pine trees. He lives in the North.

Coyote said, 'Greetings, greetings. Who are you talking about, old friend? Oh, you mean this Young-Man? He's all right though he hasn't got much sense and he doesn't appreciate fine singing. Maybe you ought to give him a Gift, seeing you are the Give-Away Chief. He needs some Gifts, he isn't much use the way he is!'

Young-Man was too frightened to be angry at this!

Buffalo Bull leaned over the top of his ridge and blew his breath over Young-Man. It smelt sweet as the South Wind across the prairie. Young-Man felt strange. He felt different now. He bowed his head and said, 'Thank you, thank you, Grandfather.'

Coyote laughed. 'Maybe he's different now, maybe he's learning something. Have you learned something, Young-Man?'

'I don't know,' said Young-Man unhappily. 'I don't know . . .'

'Maybe you'll like my singing now. How sweetly I sing! How sweetly. I think I'll just sing a bit more. Awooo, ahwooooo, ahhhwwooooooo.'

Young-Man shook his head and squinted his eyes, which had gone all misty. Suddenly he felt cold, his body was stiff, he was starving and thirsty. He was back in his hole on the mountain. The East was brightening before his drowsy eyes, and he knew the night was gone. All was still yet he seemed to hear Coyote's song still, very faint and far-off, fading away as he listened. 'Ahhwooooooo . . .'

He shrugged his shoulders in the pit and sang the little morning song to make sure his shadow would find its way back to him after wandering all night. Then he raised his arms and sang the proper song to greet the sunrise. He took off the robe and folded it neatly before laying it on the grass for the day. He took the water and sipped a little, very quietly and gratefully and carefully for he understood he would need it more and more as time went by. He thought and thought about what had happened as the sun rose higher and the day grew warmer. Sometimes he chanted little songs to himself but mostly he thought about men and all the other peoples who shared the world with men. Perhaps he was learning something. Perhaps Buffalo Bull had given him a Gift.

In the middle of the afternoon Young-Man was

dozing and feeling very hungry and thirsty when Mouse came again. Mouse seemed bigger today, as big as a rabbit. His head was over the top of the tussocks.

'Hullo, Young-Man, hullo! Do you still want to chase me? Do you still want to make me jump through the grass so you can laugh at me?'

'No, Mouse, I don't want to chase you any more. I am sorry I was cruel when I was a Small-Boy. I didn't really want to frighten you. I mean . . . well, I suppose I did want to frighten you, but now I'm sorry.'

'Oh, you've learned something,' said Mouse, sniffing hard with his bare, pink nose. 'You smell different today, you have a little whiff of Buffalo Bull about you! Maybe you are learning something after all.'

'I have listened to Old Coyote singing; I have met Buffalo Bull,' said Young-Man proudly.

'Oh, you've been talking to those Old Men, have you? You have to be careful of them; they have strange powerful songs, they are very wise.'

'What would a Mouse know about wisdom?' asked Young-Man huffily. 'I think you're jealous, that's all. Jealous because I have been talking to such big new friends. You're jealous, jealous, *jealous*! I think I *will* chase you for that!'

He struggled and struggled to get out of the hole, but he couldn't. Mouse laughed and laughed but wouldn't come close enough to be reached. Oh, no.

'I'm going away now, Young-Man. You haven't learned enough yet; I'll just leave you there.'

'You just wait till I'm free!' shouted Young-Man, but it was no use. Mouse went slowly away, looking back over his shoulder and chuckling in a most aggravating manner.

At last evening came and Young-Man took up the robe and wrapped it around his body. He sipped a little of the water. He tried to think of Buffalo Bull and Coyote, but it was no use – all he could think about was grilled rib-bones and roast hump-meat and boiled deer-flesh. But he did remember to say goodnight to the world.

'Goodnight, mountains. I am watching you swallow the sun. Look after me when darkness comes, I'm a good man, I'm not causing any trouble. Goodnight Evening Star person, goodnight rocks and grass people, I am not here to fight, I am just resting among you. Goodnight Eagle, soaring up there like a speck above me; you can see me better than I can see you. Goodnight, world. Keep me safe till the sun comes again.'

Suddenly, Eagle who had been flying so high dropped like a snowflake in winter toward the prairie, and in the light of the last ray of the sun it landed on top of a dead tree close to Young-Man, gripping with its terrible feet and glaring with its cold, golden eye. Young-Man shivered before that eye and the power that glared from it. He said, 'Eagle, have you come to talk to me? I will listen to you.'

Eagle said nothing, just went on looking.

'Eagle, have you anything to tell me?'

Eagle said nothing, just went on looking.

Young-Man got angry again. 'Oh, go away. If you haven't come to talk to me then I don't want you here laughing at me; stuck in this hole and not able to get out, so even mice can jeer at me. Cold, hungry, thirsty and lonely, too. Why don't you go away? Oh, I'll hunt you when I get out of here, just you wait and see!'

At last Eagle spoke, 'You can't See, can you. You can't See anything. Even if you could, you wouldn't Understand, would you. Poor you! Heeheeheehee-heeheehee.' Eagle laughed so mockingly and irritatingly while he watched Young-Man closely with his cold, golden eye.

'Oh, go away, go away!'

'I don't think I will. I'll just stay here and laugh at you!'

Nobody likes to be laughed at, and Young-Man was already hungry and thirsty and angry and cold. He became angry, as angry as he had been at Coyote the night before. His body strained so hard to be free to attack Eagle that suddenly – *thok* – it happened again. He was free! Not only was he free, but he could fly. He sprang into the air and flew toward Eagle. With a last thin, scream of laughter, Eagle sped off through the high, golden air toward the east. Young-Man sped in pursuit. The prairie fled by below them, and at last the plains ended near a great river and the land below changed to forests and lakes. Still they went on, Eagle laughing ahead and Young-Man furiously chasing him. Then Eagle thinned and vanished like smoke in the wind. Young-Man was left alone, and at once began to fall. He fell into a deep lake. How icy the water was, and how coldly the night wind blew! Luckily he could swim well and was soon on the sandy shore. Through the trees lining the banks he saw a little fire burning.

He set off shivering through the trees and found

that the fire was burning outside a little shelter. There was an old Grandmother Woman sitting there putting hot stones into a pot of cornmeal mush so it boiled and bubbled and cooked. She did not look up but she knew he was there for she called, 'Come here, grandson. Your food is ready.'

Young-Man went hesitantly toward her. He had forgotten his anger with the plunge into the water, and he was cold and hungry. The Grandmother Woman took some of the porridge and put it in a bowl which she handed him. He ate in silence till the bowl was empty and his stomach rejoiced with warmth and fullness.

'Who are you, Grandmother? Why have you fed me? How did you know I was coming? Were you waiting for me to arrive? Thanks, thanks for the porridge, I was hungry. Thanks, thanks for the warmth of your fire, I was cold.'

The Grandmother smiled at him. 'So many questions! From such a Young-Man, too! I am always here with my food and my fire for Young-Men if they need them; and often they come to visit me when they have learned to See a little. Otherwise they can't find the way here. Did you come peacefully with quiet in your heart?'

Young-Man hung his head. 'I was angry, I was chasing after an Eagle person because he laughed at me. Now I am sorry for I feel ashamed of my anger.'

Old Grandmother Woman smiled. 'Young-Men are often angry until they learn to See better. Then they become ashamed. Here, take this blanket, here you can sleep safe and warm.' She handed him a blanket made from elk-skins. He went into the shelter

Many Kinds of Magic

and wrapped himself warmly and slept. He had many questions still but decided to ask the Grandmother Woman for the answers in the morning.

When he woke he was cold and hungry and shivering and thirsty and back in his hole on top of the mountain, and he wondered and wondered at what he had seen and heard. Once more he spent a day of great discomfort and hardship. His water was almost gone and it took great control not to gulp the remaining drops and be done with it. Later in the afternoon Mouse came again to visit with him; and this time Mouse was as tall as a mountain lion and his colour had changed to a beautiful pale green. He came laughing and jesting up to the opening in the ground where he could see Young-Man's face peering over the edge. That face was very thin, sweat had cut clean channels down the dirt which clung to the cheeks.

'How are you, Young-Man? Are you well? Are you hungry? Are you thirsty? Are you calm and quiet in the heart? Would you still like to chase me like you chased Coyote, like you chased Eagle? Have you learned anything yet? Has anyone come to see you yet? Anyone important, I mean? You said you expected someone big and important. Have you learned to think? Have you learned to See?'

Young-Man smiled at Mouse very wearily. 'Perhaps the Person who is speaking is someone big and important,' he said politely. 'Perhaps the Person who has come to see me has something he wishes to say?'

Mouse looked at him very hard. He said, 'You can See more, I think. The first day you couldn't see past the earth and roots and tussocks. Yesterday you could see a little better, over the tops of the tussocks. Today you can see the far mountains. Maybe one day you will be able to see the view from their summits.'

'If ever that happens, dear Mouse, it will be a long, long time from now. Meanwhile, what about yourself? Are you well? Is all well with your family? Are you hungry, are you thirsty? I am sorry I cannot offer you food but I have a little water here. Would you like to drink?'

Mouse peered hard at Young-Man then said, 'Thank you, thank you, I will drink.' He took the offered water and almost drained the container so only a few drops remained. The sun sank so only its top half could be seen above the western peaks.

Mouse said, 'I must go. I have things to do and things to care for and things to see and things to think. Rest well, Young-Man. Are you *quite sure* you don't want to chase me any more?'

'I will always hunt for you from now on, but not to see you jump from tussock to tussock in fear,' said Young-Man hoarsely, for his throat was dry. 'Goodnight, Mouse. Goodnight, world, and all the Peoples in it, furred and flying and finned and naked. I am resting here, I mean no one any harm. Goodnight sun, when you rise tomorrow my time here will be done. How sweet it has been to feel your warmth and see your light. Goodnight, earth and rock and grass, keep me safe through the darkness.' By the time he had ended his goodnights his voice was only a croak through dryness.

He wrapped the cloak around him again and settled to rest. He tried to keep from thinking of running

Many Kinds of Magic

water and deep pools of coolness and sparkling shallows glinting in sunlight by watching Evening Star shining softly. He was startled to hear a deep cough just behind his head. He turned and was horrified to see it was a huge Grizzly Bear who had come up silently behind him and was squatting there on great haunches watching him closely.

'You are Young-Man? I have heard about you,' said Grizzly in his deep growl. 'Coyote has told me about you. Buffalo has told me about you. Eagle mentioned your name and old Grandmother Woman said you had been to visit her. Mouse also says he has spoken with you. Is all this true? Have you seen all these people? Will you try to chase me as you chased them? I don't run, you know. I wait. All the time I wait. I am the one who is there when you least expect to meet me. I am the one who is waiting for you when you have dropped exhausted after running away. I am in your head, Young-Man, and you are in my head.'

'What do you want with me?' asked Young-Man weakly, for he was terribly afraid and his voice was failing from dryness.

'I want you to come with me.'

'I can't get out of this hole,' said Young-Man hopefully because he did not want to go.

'You got out for Coyote. You got out for Eagle. Now you must get out for me!'

Young-Man sighed and wished but there was no escape. He strained and struggled and at last – *thok* – he stood beside Bear on the cold hillside.

Bear said, 'Are you a good person? Are you a give-away person? Otherwise you cannot climb on my back; you will fall off.'

Young-Man thought for a moment, then he said, 'I gave Mouse a drink of water.'

'That's good, that's good. Climb up, then.'

He climbed the great shaggy side and settled his knees behind the huge shoulders. Bear began to run; swiftly, speedily, faster and faster so he seemed to fly; and always he ran toward the faint glow that marked the place in the sky where the sun had gone behind the peaks when it set. As they sped along, the last glow faded and they went on through thick darkness. The stars vanished and Young-Man knew they had run into the entrance of an enormous cave. Faint echoes of Bear's running feet rang back at them from distant walls and roof – patterpatterpatterpatter – and at last Bear halted.

'I must leave you here, Young-Man. Remember all you have learned from your friends and you will be safe,' he said. Then he was soundlessly gone. It was as if he had never been. All was silent save for the faint beat of a distant drumming, beating an endless rhythm.

No fleck or glint or gleam of light had penetrated here, no starlight or sun, no soft moon-glow or fire-light. The air around Young-Man was thick and heavy as pitchy dust. It seemed to fill his nostrils and mouth and ears and press against his open eyes.

He stood motionless at the centre of the fog of darkness, listening to the drumbeat. He was aware that some great power was coming toward him through the dark, though how he knew this was a mystery to him. Then a deep voice sounded in his head like the low rumble of distant thunder around far-off peaks.

> *This Young-Man went hunting Something, but he*
> *was foolish and angry,*
> *This Young-Man hunted though his eyes were closed,*
> *This Young-Man was dull and stupid when he set*
> *out to hunt.*
> *He found his quarry, he found what he was looking*
> *for,*
> *Will he know it when he Sees it, when he grasps it,*
> *Will he be brave enough to keep it, the Thing he*
> *hunted?*
> *What shall we do with this Young-Man?*

Young-Man stood silent, for he was afraid. Another softer voice took up the words:

> *Perhaps he has learned something, perhaps he Sees,*
> *Let us hear what this Young-Man has to say.*

Then there was a silent waiting that was more frightening than the voices had been. Young-Man took his courage in his hands, and suddenly he remembered all the people who had spoken to him in the past two days. He found his voice and it rang clear in the blackness as a bone whistle, for bravery was in his heart, lighting it as lightning flares in the heart of a great storm-cloud.

> *I have no lance, I have no bow, he sang*
> *I climb jagged rocks under a storm of hail, naked*
> *and weaponless.*

I sit on the mountain naked, crying for power,
Oh, my people, my friends,
Mouse, Coyote, Buffalo, Eagle, Bear –
Where have you gone? Why have you left me?
You are still with me, you are in my heart
And I am not afraid.
If this is the time for me to die
Then I leave my love for Old Grandmother
Woman,
For my family, for my grandfather, for my uncles,
for the People.
For the Eagle trackless through the air,
For the snake trackless among the rocks,
For the fish trackless in the lakes,
For the spirits trackless on the wind.
That is all I have to say. It is finished!

In his heart he wondered where he found those words, but he knew they were true words.

The drum stopped beating and he was alone in the thick dark; cold and hungry and thirsty and brave, but he wasn't lonely any more.

Then Young-Man felt a hand on his shoulder and the curtains lifted from his eyes. It was his grandfather's hand, it was shaking him gently. He was back in his hole on the mountain and the sun was rising. Wordlessly the old man gave him a drink of water. As a little of his strength returned he was gently helped from the hole and led to where his father and uncles were waiting. Then they took him back to the camp where he ate and rested.

When he was quite recovered he told his grandfather every word that had been spoken and everything that had happened to him. The old man looked at him with eyes that twinkled.

'What do you think now?' he asked. 'Was it a good hunt? Are you still bored? Will you still wander around looking for something? Did you catch anything?'

Young-Man grinned at the old man. He said, 'It was a good hunt. Now another hunt begins. I will take my weapons and travel to many places to see many things and talk and listen to many people. When I come back from that hunt maybe I'll know more than I know now!'

'That's good! That's good! You won't be called Young-Man any more now, you'll have a new name. You will be called Man-Who-Travels, and all the people will respect you.'

Man-Who-Travels laughed loud and long at this saying. 'People can call me whatever they like,' he said, 'but my real name will always be Man-Who-Learned-From-Mouse.'

His father and uncles and grandfather laughed with him then. 'Well, what will you be?' asked the uncles. 'Will you be a crazy man, a care-for-nothing man, a fighter, a hunter to feed the people, a doctor to cure the people, or a chief to lead the people?'

'I will be all those things,' said Man-Who-Travels.

And that is only the beginning of his story.

THE BUNYIP
WHO DIDN'T LIKE PEOPLE

There was this young bunyip in the old days, and none of the other bunyips would talk to him. Bunyips in the Murray and the Coorong and the Blue Lake and Lake Alexandrina and everywhere else used to eat people. Everybody said they were pretty wicked creatures. Especially the people whose friends had been eaten by them. But the bunyips didn't care, they liked eating people.

This young bunyip didn't like the taste of people. When he was a little pup bunyip, his mother used to say, 'Come along, dear. Do try this nice piece of shepherd.'

Sometimes his father would shout, 'You're not to leave the table until you've finished that bit of Aboriginal right up! If you don't, you'll get it again for your tea!' But the young bunyip still wouldn't eat people. He only liked water-weeds and fruit. He must have been the first vegetarian bunyip ever.

When he grew big enough to leave home, he said, 'Mother and Father, you don't understand me. I am going off to find a river where I can live the way I want to. Where people won't tell me what to do all the time. Goodbye.'

So he oozed up the bank about where Murray Bridge is now and flippered off toward the west. His mother was unhappy for a while and missed him. But his father said, 'Ungrateful cub! He will learn his lesson. He will be glad to come back some day when he is hungry and lonely!'

'Oh, dear! Do you think he will get hungry and lonely?' asked Mother Bunyip.

'Here, my dear, don't be so sad. Young people must learn,' said Father. 'Here, have a piece of this grazier. He's delicious!'

After a time the mother grew used to not having her child home in their nice slimy hole under the riverbank. Sometimes at night though when the wind was howling cheerfully and the rain was belting down, she would say, 'What a shame our child isn't here to enjoy this delightful weather with us.' Then she would lift her heads above the water and call out mournfully till people thought a paddle steamer was coming. But the little bunyip didn't come back.

When he left the delicious mud of the Murray, he had travelled all night. When dawn came, he had hidden from the nasty sunlight and ugly blue sky under the friendly smile of an old waterhole. So he kept going, travelling from waterhole to lagoon. At last he came one dawn to a great big water-hole full of the slipperiest, scummiest water he had ever seen.

'What a lovely place!' he said as he slid down the clay bank into the long, slimy fronds of the water-weeds. He began feeding happily and humming to himself at the same time. This musical noise (which sounded rather like a shovel scraping on a concrete

Many Kinds of Magic

floor) attracted the attention of an old gentleman bunyip who had lived there a long time. He oozed out of his attractively boggy cave. Then he hunted through the murky water until he found the youngster.

'Welcome to the Bremer River, m'boy,' he grunted cheerfully. 'You're the first visitor I've had for simply ages. What's the news?'

'Well, I've left home because my parents don't understand me. Now I'm looking for a home where I can do my own thing,' said the young bunyip. He spoke with one of his mouths while he went on shovelling weeds down his other necks.

'My parents didn't understand me, either. I say, young feller, don't fill yourself up with all that salad. There's a swagman camped at the northern end you can have for a second course! I'd eat him myself but I ate two bullocks last night. My indigestion is giving me trouble. I've got a weak stomach, and those hoofs and horns are hard to digest.' Then it burped politely behind one of his flippers. 'Pardon me, I'm sure.'

'Thank you for your kind offer, but I can't eat people. Never could. They make me feel ill. I'd rather just stick to vegetables,' said the young bunyip. He squirted water from one of his mouths to blow some lovely brown muck on to his weed before stuffing it in and chewing it.

'Don't eat people! You don't eat people?' roared the old bunyip. 'Bunyips have always eaten people! It's part of our way of life! You'd better leave, I think. Can't have young upstarts here, eating weeds and not a proper diet! You're letting our side down, young feller!'

'Sorry,' burbled the young bunyip. 'Well, you don't understand me either. I suppose I'll just have to keep travelling. Do you mind if I stay for the day? You wouldn't turn even a stockman out under that horrible blue sky and dreadful sunlight. Please let me stay until tonight.'

'Oh, very well. But don't you go to the other end of the waterhole and frighten my snack away!' roared the old bunyip.

He scuttled slimily away through the slippery, lovely mud, bubbling things like: 'Don't know what the world's coming to!' and 'Young people today reckon they know more than their elders!' Things like that. But the youngster didn't care. He just tucked his heads under his flippers and rolled into a soft, leathery ball. He drifted off to sleep under a friendly, black, rotten tree-trunk on the bottom.

It was a lovely night when he set out again. The wind howled among the trees. Rain pelted on the ground, and all was squishy. The young bunyip hurried along. Just before daylight he came to a rather small river full of water. He slid down the bank and under the water just as the east turned red with the coming sun. There were no other bunyips living there at all.

Here the young bunyip made his home. He dug a big cave under the bank and decorated it with lovely green slime, dead fish and old bones. Although he was a vegetarian, he still liked a bit of art on his walls. How deliciously ugly they looked!

★

Many Kinds of Magic

It was a lonely life for him for the first couple of years. The river rose and ran strongly in winter. It dried to a trickle in summer, but he was very comfortable. Sometimes he got a bit lonely and thought he might go and visit his parents. Then he thought how his father would nag him, so he didn't go. The fish and turtles didn't have much conversation. They just used to say, 'Good day, mate,' as they swam past. They didn't seem to care whether he answered or not.

One lovely day in winter when the rain had poured all day and the freezing wind roughed the surface, the bunyip thought he heard something. It was a voice singing a duet with itself. He hastily swam toward the noise and was delighted to find that it came from a young lady bunyip. She was beautiful. Her big, blood-shot eyes glowed in the muddy water. Her long, sharp teeth stuck right out of her mouth. And her leathery skin was covered with bright green slime that looked as though it hadn't been disturbed for years.

The bunyip was thrilled to have company. The lady bunyip told him she had come there from another little river. Her parents didn't understand her, either. They insisted that she ate some settlers that were planting vineyards on the hills. They had very big feet and didn't taste nice at all. The young bunyip told her how good it was to be a vegetarian.

After a little while she decided she loved him. She came to live with him in his lovely home under the bank. A few years after this they had a small girl bunyip. They named her Onkaparinga after the river where they lived.

For many years the little family lived happily. They snorted and puffed and hooted at night. They rolled happily all the way from Mount Torrens to Port Noarlunga and back again. Life was carefree for them until one day when their little girl was nearly grown up. On this day their teenage bunyip was trying a little sea bathing at Christies Beach. She didn't like it much because the salt water hurt her eyes and made her squint. She saw something twinkling in the water ahead of her. There were two big feet with bunions, two thin legs like drinking straws with knobby hinges on them, and the bottom end of a blue bathing suit. Absent-mindedly she inhaled them.

That night when she got home to the cave, she said to her parents, 'There is a really new, delicious taste thrill out in the salt water! It has big feet, thin legs and wears a sort of blue thing you have to spit out afterwards.'

Her parents turned white under their green skins. Her father said, 'Wretched child! That was a people! You have eaten a people! Don't you know that is why your mother and I came to live here? So that we wouldn't have to eat any more people like your grandparents do! Shame on you, girl!'

'Do you mean to say you have never told me this?' asked the girl bunyip.

'We know what is best for you,' said her father. 'You must promise never to eat a people ever again.'

'You don't understand me,' said the daughter. 'I am going to run away and live with Grandfather and Grandmother in the Murray River.' So she did.

Her grandparents made her very welcome. Grandfather kept saying, 'Breeding will tell.' He never said what he meant by this.

She lives with them still. I wouldn't advise you to swim in the Murray River, friends, although you'll be pretty safe in most places these days. Of course you'll always be safe in the Onkaparinga River unless you are carelessly in the middle of a big clump of weeds. Then you might get swallowed by accident. But it comes to the same thing, doesn't it? So watch out!

BLACK BEETLE

There was once a Black Beetle who lived with her family and friends and relatives among the roots of a giant tree. The tree stood just where the tangled, deep, spiny jungle of the Congo thinned and gave way to the golden grasslands of the Plains. Black Beetle was so small you could not see her among the dead leaves and twigs and bits of bark littering the ground under the massive tree. Her wing-cases were exactly the colour of the very best treacle toffee; and when she lifted them to fly, her wings were a most beautiful crimson. Yet though she was beautiful she was not happy. She was afraid of Golden Bird who lived high in the branches of the tree and ate Black Beetles!

One day when she was wailing and lamenting her uneasy life her crying was heard by a small Brown Ghost who happened to be passing. (He was just starting his holidays. Small Brown Ghosts are allowed six days holiday after every hundred years of haunting.) He was on his way to cool his feet in a little stream that flowed from the jungle and out on to the hot grasslands.

When he heard Beetle crying he stopped. He could hear her thin voice but he couldn't see who was making the noise. He looked carefully until he found her, hiding under a fallen leaf, for Brown Ghosts have keen sight. Taking her gently on the palm of one shivery hand, he asked her the cause of her sorrow.

'It is Golden Bird. She eats Black Beetles! We think she must be the strongest thing in the world. If we forget about her for just one second she swoops and eats us,' explained Beetle. Brown Ghost was fascinated. 'Do you really think she is so powerful?' he asked. 'I'll tell you what; let's go together to Golden Bird and see what she has to say. Don't be afraid, she would never dare eat you if you are with me. I'll protect you.'

Beetle hesitated; but it seemed to her that here was a chance to see more of the world than dead leaves, twigs and grass-roots, so she agreed. Brown Ghost closed his fingers gently so she was safely held then drifted to the tree-top where Golden Bird swung to and fro on a thin twig, singing like a flute and watching the ground intently for her dinner.

'Golden Bird, Golden Bird, I have brought Black Beetle to visit you. She thinks you are the most powerful thing in the world. Are you?'

'Oh, no! Tweetle tee, oh no! Bush Cat is the most powerful thing in the world! Teedle wee sweet treat!' Golden Bird looked carefully about her as she spoke and sang. The sun glistened on her feathery wings and back so they shone and gleamed exactly like the stone called tiger-eye.

Brown Ghost said to Black Beetle, 'You see? You

see? Golden Bird isn't the most powerful thing at all.'

'What is a Bush Cat?' asked Beetle.

Golden Bird heard her. 'Oh, don't you know about Bush Cat? You are very lucky. He's the cruellest, hungriest, quietest thief in the world, you see see see see see. He creeps and sneaks and slips along on his pawful of prickles and he peers and stares from his shining eyes. Oh, my poor nest, and oh, my poor children; he'd eat eat eat eat eat us all if he could find us and catch us. He'd chew me in his chops and toss me with his claws and dance with my poor corpus if ever he caught me, and I think it's a pity pity pity pity pity, don't you?'

Black Beetle said softly to Brown Ghost, 'I think I'd like to see Bush Cat. Anyone as powerful as that deserves a look. Please, will you take me? I feel safe if you are with me.'

'I'll take you, I'll take you,' laughed Brown Ghost, peering down at her with his wispy eye. 'I'd like to see this dreadful creature myself!' So off they drifted to find Bush Cat.

He was in a little clearing, playing with some feathers that blew idly in the wind. First he lay on his back, tossing them from soft paw to soft paw; then he sprang high in the air to hit them with his thorny claws; then he pretended to be afraid of them and flew across the clearing as lightly and silently as though he was a piece of fluff himself.

'Bush Cat, Bush Cat, Golden Bird says you are the most powerful thing in the world,' said Brown Ghost.

'Perhaps I am, perhaps I am!' said Bush Cat proudly.

The sun shone clear on his yellow coat and white belly, and on the stripes that striped him and the blotches that mottled him. When he stood still in the stippled light of the leaves and grasses you could barely see him.

'Come out where we can see your beauty,' commanded Brown Ghost.

'I mustn't get too far from the trees,' said Bush Cat nervously. 'It's Wild Dog, you know. He chases me, but he can't climb.'

'If you are so powerful, why are you so afraid of Wild Dog?' asked Black Beetle with great interest.

'Because he is a bully and a biter, a snarler and a fighter, and he hates Bush Cats more than anything.'

At that very instant Wild Dog burst from the bushes shouting 'Urrrrrrgh! Row row row row row row row. Grrrrowwwwwwll!' Before the first growl, it seemed, Bush Cat was three metres high in the branches of a tree spitting in the rudest way you can imagine.

'Downdowndowndowndown! Come down and fight!' roared Wild Dog.

'Spitttttttsss-foo! Shan't! Weeeeee-how! Spittttttz!' said Bush Cat.

'Oh, my chains and groans, what a noise!' said Brown Ghost. 'Hush, oh hush, the both of you. Now, here I have a small friend, a tiny handsome friend who is looking for the most powerful thing in the world. Do you think it might be you, Wild Dog?'

Wild Dog was delighted. His front end grinned

all sharp and white and pointed, and his back end waved from side to side. He looked up at Brown Ghost in a most friendly manner.

'I'm not one to boast, but everyone runs away when they see me coming,' he said proudly.

'*Huh*!!' hissed Bush Cat. 'What about the day before yesterday! Down at the drinking pool! Down comes proud, proud Wild Dog! *But* Old Buffalo Bull was there, rolling and soaking in the squidgey mud. Wild Dog looked at the rippled horns and the staring eyes and thick wrinkly hide, and what did he do, this powerful one? Trembled! That's what he did! Trembled, then ran!'

'Nownownownownownownow!' roared Wild Dog furiously, but Black Beetle could see he was embarrassed.

Brown Ghost looked consideringly at Wild Dog. 'Old Buffalo Bull. Has he got more power than you, then?'

'Aaaaaaaaaaaagrh, yes he has,' growled Wild Dog. 'But I'll bite Bush Cat for saying so!'

'Spitttttttz-eow! Put away your sharp and shining fangs, old Blunt Claws. Climb and catch me first,' said Bush Cat.

Black Beetle and Brown Ghost left Wild Dog doing his war-dance around and around the tree where Bush Cat crouched just beyond his reach, shouting dreadful things at one another at the same time.

Soon the noise was dulled by the distance.

'What now? Old Buffalo Bull, do you think?'

'If you don't mind, please, Ghost. I'd like to see the beast who has more power than Wild Dog.'

'Oh, I don't mind, little one. What a lot of strange

things we are seeing, to be sure.'

They went on together, the drifting shape and the tiny, shining speck of jet cuddled safe in his hand. By and by they came to the wallows and grunt-holes near the drinking pool where Old Buffalo Bull spent most of his time when he wasn't out filling his great belly with the grass of the Plains. They could see his wide horns wrinkling above the muddy ooze, and when they stopped close by he opened his eyes wide to stare at them. Buffalo Bull looks sleepy and drowsy and caught up in a dream, but he isn't! Not even a ghost can creep up on him without being noticed.

'Whooooo are youuuuu looking for?' he mooed and rumbled.

'Pardon for waking you, Lord of the Herds,' said Brown Ghost respectfully, for he was well brought up and knew polite things to say. 'My friend here is looking for the most powerful thing in the world, and Wild Dog says that he always makes way for you. Are you the one my friend is seeking?'

Buffalo considered this for a long time. A foolish person might have thought that he had gone back to sleep but Brown Ghost knew better than that.

After a time Old Buffalo Bull opened his eyes again and said, 'Of the eaters of grass; zebra, eland and the rest, none cross my path or argue with me. Even Old Rhino lets me be. But I must tell the truth, for good people are honest. There is one to whom I bow, and when we meet on the path I stand aside.'

'Not . . . *Lion?*' whispered Black Beetle, and though she spoke softly Buffalo heard her.

Many Kinds of Magic

'No, little one; not Lion, though he has power, too. The one I mean is the Mountain That Walks, the Silent One, thruster down of thorn trees, swayer in shady places.'

'Old Elephant!' said Beetle, and Buffalo nodded a little.

'Old Elephant,' he agreed. 'The truly powerful one, for he spares others despite his power. Look for him, little one.'

When Buffalo said this, all the little birds who sat on his back to chase his ticks nodded and chattered in agreement. Old Bull closed his eyes again and wriggled lower in the slush and ooze and sludge that filled his wallow.

'Well, little sister, what shall we do now?' asked Brown Ghost cheerfully. 'Shall we follow this trail to its end?'

'Please yes, if you are not too tired,' said Beetle.

'Tired? I have no body so I never get tired! Also this is much better sport than frightening fat people with my spooky moans. By all means let us go and seek Elephant.'

They went to the border of the forest where it turns from jungle to clearing, from tangle to open plains. There was Elephant and all her family in a shady place. They loomed like a range of mountains and swayed backwards and forwards like the waves of the ocean, and no sound was heard from them at all but the rumbling from their insides as they digested their dinners.

Ghost went straightaway to the oldest Granny. She was huge and wrinkled and grey as a rain cloud in the Wet Season when rain comes to the Plains.

One of her long tusks was broken, and her eyes were tiny and wise.

'Grandmother, this friend of mine wishes to find the most powerful thing in the world. We have looked for a long time and now our journey has brought us here,' said Brown Ghost, very respectfully.

Old Granny nodded her huge head so her ears flapped and her trunk swayed but she said nothing.

'Are you the strongest thing in the world?' shouted Black Beetle.

Granny Elephant nodded and kept her mouth closed. Brown Ghost smiled a little.

'Is there nothing that makes you run away? Nothing at all?' he asked.

The great old Grandmother looked at him suspiciously. Then, in a soft rumbling voice like a distant thunder-roll she said, 'There is Fire Himself. When his children dance in the long brown grass at the end of the Dry Season, everybody – everybody from silly Weaverbird to Old Grumble-Rhino, from shining black Mamba with his cheeks full of poison to Very Silent Giraffe – all run and run. We all flee crackling grass and choking smoke and red, biting embers. That has always been the way of things.'

'Then Fire Himself is stronger, since you fly from it,' said Ghost.

The old one swayed and nodded silently, feeling under her with her trunk to make sure her grandson was safe. She was looking after him while his mother went for a drink.

Brown Ghost thanked Granny respectfully, and the two friends left the silent, swaying herd.

'Where now? To see Fire Himself? His children are everywhere but He lives in a mountain far away. It will be a long journey. Shall we go to Fire, little one?'

'Yes please, dear friend,' said Black Beetle; and they went.

Brown Ghost drifted and sped on the face of the wind, and after a long time Beetle saw they were coming to a mountain. Part of the mountain was snow, but part was on fire and from a gash in the side there rolled torrents of cherry-red melted stone that slowed as it cooled on its sluggish journey downhill. In the crater from whence it came lived Fire Himself. From here he sent out his children who lived far away on the Plains and in the Jungles. These children boiled men's pots and smelted their spearheads. Sometimes one would escape and speed across the Plains, as Elephant said; but all of them were parts of Fire Himself who lived in his volcano.

Brown Ghost strode fearlessly to the very rim of the crater and looked down where melted stone heaved and bubbled like maize porridge in a pot.

'Hey! Ohay, Fire! It is I, Brown Ghost who call you!'

A wisp of smoke rose from the troubled furnace and hung before them. A thin voice was heard to say, 'Go away. I am resting. In 341 years from now I shall rise up and bury the lakes and trees with ashes and eruption. Just now I am resting. I am a sleeping volcano. Do not disturb me!'

'Elephant says your children are mightier than she is and that they are the only thing in the world from which she runs!'

'That is true, but surely you didn't disturb me to tell me that. All the world knows that already!'

'Tell us, master of fire and stone, is there nothing stronger than you? Stronger than your children? My friend is looking for the strongest thing in the world.'

Fire thought for a time in silence, then said, 'Here in my home there is nothing that bothers me. But out in the world my children fear water, for when they meet with it they die, every time. I must speak truly and say that water is stronger than my children, and even sends spies to my very doorstep to watch me! See, that snow up there is water, but we shall see what happens in just another 341 years. Oho, just wait!'

Deep in the mountain under their feet there was a roaring and a rumbling, a turning and thundering and tumbling, and out from the lake of boiling stone came enormous, red-hot boulders to be tossed into the air like feathers in a whirlwind. Brown Ghost closed his hand protectively around Black Beetle and they fled on the face of the wind.

A safe distance away they slowed and settled on top of a rocky, rounded hill where things were much safer and a lot more comfortable.

'Shaahh! This is a long journey, little one,' he said at last.

'Perhaps we should go home,' suggested Beetle humbly. She trembled, remembering Fire Himself. She had never been so afraid before, even when Golden Bird was singing and pecking close by her hiding-place. Brown Ghost shook his shimmery head. 'We have come so far, let us go on to the end,' he said. 'We will go to Water.'

They sped along until they came to a long white sandy beach set between high, rocky headlands where more water than Beetle had ever imagined swooped and rushed and sucked back, only to tower, fall, swoop and rush back again. She was afraid, but she bravely stayed in Ghost's hand when he walked to the edge of the waves and shouted, 'Water! Hey, Water! Fire Himself says that you are stronger than he is. You easily quench his children. Are you the strongest thing in the world?'

There came a hush in the rushing and a stillness in the foaming, then a voice so deep that it trembled and vibrated through the bodies of the friends, said, 'I am strong – strong. I wear away stone. I eat into earth. I chew and bite the feet of mountains and am never weary. Yet Sun is stronger. He dries me up, he takes my body and turns it into clouds; they travel to far places and see strange things before they turn to rain and fall and so return to me to tell me strange stories. Yes, Sun is stronger, though I am strong.'

'Of course, that's it at last!' shouted Black Beetle. 'Whyever didn't we think of that? Sun, our Lord, our Master, our father, must be the most powerful thing anywhere. He can defeat water, and water is indeed mighty.'

The two looked and peered and studied and observed and admired water. There was the shift in colours, from deepest indigo on the face of the horizon deeps, changing to blue and green and pale crystal as the shore shelved and shallowed. There was the pellucid stillness of rock pools and lagoons. There was the brilliance of gems where the waves dashed the rocks, flinging spray like diamonds and moonstones and jargoons. There was whiteness like the egret's plumes where foam streaked broken water. Water was great to behold, enormous, restless, powerful. Yet water bowed to Sun!

'We must go to Sun, then, for our answer,' said Brown Ghost, and set off.

When they reached Sun's home it took all the power and magic and skill of Brown Ghost to save them from being crisped by his power. Yet they went bravely forward, and Sun drew a darkness across his face and asked them what they wanted. He was mostly a kindly force, and loved his many children who swam and walked and leapt and flew on the earth far below. They told him their search and the reason why they had come to him.

He laughed. 'Some say I am powerful, and indeed in the deserts few can stand against me; but consider, my children, my beloved pets. Though I may shine fiercely, yet there is one who overcomes my power!'

'Who may that be, lord?' asked Brown Ghost humbly.

'Why, clouds, of course! I may dry water up, but he has his revenge when his children mask my light! Perhaps clouds are mightier than I am. Why don't you go and ask them?'

When they came to the place of clouds they were astonished at the number and sizes and varieties of the Cloud People. Some were long and thin and straight, some rounded and soft as feathers, some were black-featured and angry with fire and thunder in their hearts, while others were tiny and rounded and pink.

'Yes, we can block Sun from shining on the Jungle and the Plains,' they said when Brown Ghost asked them. 'But you forget that we have a master who overcomes us easily. Perhaps he is the most powerful, for he moves us though we do overcome Sun.'

'Who is that, who is that?' clamoured Ghost.

'Wind, of course,' grumbled a bad-tempered cumulo-nimbus. 'We must go where he sends us.'

A long flight and a strong flight took them at last to the place at the edges of the world where the winds rested. Ghost was worried as they drew near in case Hurricane might be keeping watch that day, for he was a furious fellow. When they arrived they found that Hurricane, Typhoon, Storm, Cyclone, Tempest and the rougher fellows were all asleep and the watch was being kept by gentle South Wind who comes in the Spring of the year to waken the sleeping grasses. She was a gentle, friendly person, and laughed in a kindly way when Ghost explained why the two of them were visiting.

'Perhaps it is just as well my rough brothers and sisters are not awake!' she said when she was done chuckling. 'They might claim to be the strongest things in the world. Certainly they are very strong, but one thing defeats them. Rock is sturdy and deep-rooted in the ground, and despite their maelstroms and destruction, rock stands unmoved. Even Cyclone cannot disturb Rock. Now you had better go quickly for my watch is almost ended and one rougher than I will soon be waking. You might not be safe if you stay here too long!'

They hurried off with her laughter still in their ears, and it was as well they did, for after a time a great wind seized them and tossed and jumbled them along, spinning like falling leaves. They were grateful to come to rest upon a great black rock under which grew a tall, straight tree which seemed to Black Beetle to be very familiar.

She stared at it very hard, then said, 'Well, fancy that! All my life I have been living in the shadow of the strongest thing in the world, for this rock is one I know, and that is my very own tree where I was born and grew up!'

'Things are often like that,' said Brown Ghost calmly with a strange little smile. 'Power and strength are often unregarded by those who become over-familiar with them. So, Rock! You are the strongest thing in the world, eh?'

A slow, stony voice answered, 'I . . . am . . . not . . . the . . . strongest . . . thing . . . here. Tree . . . is . . . splitting . . . me . . . slowly . . . with . . . her . . . tough . . . roots. She . . . is . . . stronger!'

Then there was silence. Beetle was amazed. 'Tree? *Tree* is stronger? All my life I have lived here as grub, cocoon and beetle! I raised my family here where all is homely and familiar; yet I was living beneath the strongest thing in the world. Here is a great wonder. Tree, you are modest and brave and from now on we Black Beetles will never cease to praise you for your power and strength and shy modesty. Great, strong tree, we have travelled the world and met many Great Persons; and now we find you to be the greatest of all!'

If Black Beetle could have wept she would have wept for joy and sorrow mixed. Brown Ghost watched and listened and smiled as he grew fainter and fainter

Many Kinds of Magic

and harder to see. Beetle ended her praises of the tree and was about to creep under the dead leaf she called home when suddenly there was a green, soggy-sounding voice whispering to her and to Brown Ghost.

'Strongest? Strongest? Did you say I am strongest of all? Alas, my roots are being chewed and munched and eaten by millions of Black Beetles and their children. One day soon I must fall, fall!'

There was a deep silence as Tree finished speaking. Beetle was speechless. Brown Ghost had almost faded by this, but she could see he was grinning right across his fading face. His voice reached her very faintly for the last time.

'It's my holidays and now I'm off to cool my feet in the jungle stream. Farewell, Black Beetle, strongest, most powerful thing in the whole wide world! Or are you, little one? Are you?'

Then he faded completely from view.

GREAT-GRANDFATHER'S GHOST

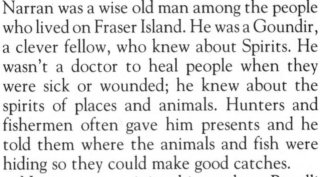

Narran was a wise old man among the people who lived on Fraser Island. He was a Goundir, a clever fellow, who knew about Spirits. He wasn't a doctor to heal people when they were sick or wounded; he knew about the spirits of places and animals. Hunters and fishermen often gave him presents and he told them where the animals and fish were hiding so they could make good catches.

Narran was training his nephew Benalli to be the same kind of clever fellow, too. Benalli was very good looking and the women admired him. He thought about this a lot when he should have been thinking about the business his old Uncle had given him to learn. Narran knew that until Benalli stopped being proud and vain he would never learn to think properly about being a clever fellow, and this saddened him.

One day the old man came to where Benalli was sitting by his fire and said, 'I have been invited to go to the bunya feast by our neighbours. People are coming from everywhere. There will be great feasting on the bunya nuts and other good food. There will be great dancing and entertainment, and some good fights to watch.'

'Can I come too?' asked Benalli.

'No. There will be a lot of visitors from the west and south and north as well as our people from the coast. You would get into trouble, chasing the girls the way you do,' said Narran. 'Anyway, I have a task for you while I'm away. Someone has to advise the people where to hunt and fish, and that will be your job until I come back.'

Benalli wasn't happy about this but he knew he would have to do as he was told. Narran took a skin bag he carried looped around his neck and said, 'In here is a spirit stone that tells me where the fish, possums and kangaroos are hiding. You must look after it carefully because the ghost of my great-grandfather lives in the stone. It is his house. All you have to do is hold the stone through the leather and it will move your hand in the right direction to send the hunters.'

'Is it as easy as that?' asked Benalli, amazed.

'The hard part is to get a spirit to come and settle there in the first place, and then to keep him there even though he might want to go somewhere else,' said Narran. 'Mind you, he doesn't want to stay in the stone in the bag, and he might try to get away from you. You must talk nicely to him, and feed him a little honey now and then. He loves honey. Now I must go, the other guests are ready to leave and it wouldn't be polite to keep them waiting.'

He handed the bag to Benalli, who hung it around his neck. Then he went off through the green bush with the other people who had been invited to the bunya feast. Benalli looked after him enviously, then resigned himself to the task the old man had set him.

For a few days Benalli acted properly, behaving modestly and politely as a young man should. When anyone asked advice he gave it but he found that the people he advised didn't give him any presents. They said they would wait till Narran came home and make the gifts to him because it was his magic that was advising them, not Benalli's. Benalli got quite angry at this and began to neglect his duties and go off hunting by himself. He always got a lot of food because great-grandfather's ghost told him where to go, but other people didn't have much success and they began to get hungry and angry with him.

One day Benalli was out at the end of a rocky point of the island with his fish spear. The bag had told him there would be good fishing there that day. He stood still as the stones around him waiting for the fish to swim by but few came. When he did cast his spear he missed every one. After a while he grew angry and unslung the bag holding the stone and said, 'You aren't doing your job very well today. You must try harder or I'll squeeze you dreadfully!'

At these words the bag gave a great leap out of his fingers and into the water. A little fish thought the bag was something nice to eat and swallowed it with a gulp. Then it dived deep and out of sight. Benalli was frantic with worry. Who knew what Narran might do to him if he came home and found his magic bag gone? He might turn Benalli into anything – a shellfish to be eaten, water for someone to drink, or even a dead stick someone might burn in the fire! Benalli dived into the water and swam hastily down after the fish. He was only a beginner at magic but he could remember the spell that made him able to breathe under the sea.

When he reached the bottom he was horrified to see many, many fish exactly like the one that had swallowed great-grandfather's ghost swimming around in the coral and seaweed. He clung to a piece of beautiful crimson staghorn coral and watched the school of little fish carefully. He soon saw one of them finding more food than the others and decided that it was this fish that contained the bag. Something was guiding it!

'That's the one,' thought Benalli happily and swam cautiously toward it, his spear poised. He was just about to catch it when a much bigger fish came round the corner of a big clump of yellow coral and swallowed the small fish. Then it swirled around and shot off into deeper water. Benalli swore bad words to himself and followed as fast as he could swim.

This fish was one that lived out where the green water began to turn deep blue, and Benalli could no longer see the ocean floor under him. There was nothing but the darkening depths. Around him was the clear blue and scattered through it were silver fish looking like stars at early evening as they flashed and turned in the light shafted down from the surface.

Luckily for Benalli the fish he was following had joined a school of its fellows, for it could swim much

Many Kinds of Magic

faster than he could and he would soon have been out-distanced. Now it was part of the swarm that hung in the water like the Milky Way on a clear sky at dusk. He had the same problem as before, but it was even more difficult, for there were many more of these fish than there had been of the smaller ones. The one he wanted had merged with all its brothers and sisters and he had lost sight of it in the school. Benalli swore again, terrible swears that came from his mouth like little bubbles and burst like clouds of steam when they reached the surface far above, frightening an old green turtle who was trying to sleep there.

The school of big fish began to slowly travel south, and Benalli had to follow. Suddenly the whole congregation of fish began to swirl in a terrified way, to swim frantically, to mill and leap above the surface. Benalli was horrified to see a huge shark swimming fast from seaward, dim in the blue at first but rapidly growing more distinct as it came closer. He could see the wide jaws and terrible triangular teeth as it rushed at the school of fish who were trying desperately to escape. To his surprise he suddenly realized that the shark was after one particular fish in the school. It was the magic of grandfather's ghost at work again! Benalli hovered as still as a piece of floating weed and watched, not wanting to draw any attention to himself in case he became dinner for the shark too.

The shark turned and twisted like lightning and at last, with a quick snap of its jaws, its quarry was gone. Then it lost interest in the rest of the school and swam seaward again, out to where the paler water was turned to the royal blue of the great deeps.

Benalli almost wept with rage and frustration. Great-grandfather must be feeling really secure now he was inside a fish inside a fish inside a shark and heading out to sea! He was cold and tired and afraid, but he dared not give up his pursuit. Who knew what would happen if he went back with this news to Narran? The old man might turn him into an oyster and eat him! He grimly set his jaw, took a firmer grip on the shaft of his spear and set off after the shark.

By swimming as fast as he could he gradually overtook the great shark, but he was tiring badly and knew with despair that he would need to be stronger than he felt if he was to spear and kill such a strong enemy. Still, he closed with it until it was almost in stabbing range. Just as he prepared to lunge he caught a flicker of something strange in the deeps beyond. At first he thought it was some great undersea rock or the lower part of an island, then he realized with horror that it was a living creature. It was moving toward them both.

The shark turned suddenly and began to flee, and so did the young man. Side by side they swam at their utmost speed away from whatever it was that pursued them. They ignored each other in their terror of their hunter. Benalli stole a quick glance across one shoulder at the thing that was overhauling them so fast. One glance was enough. That great open mouth, those serrated teeth, the enormous body – it could only be Moha-moha the monster, the sea-serpent that fed on whales and great sharks and even came ashore sometimes to hunt men! He tried to swim faster, his body even brushing unregarded against the terrible rough skin of the shark.

It was no use. A sudden current of water wafted Benalli backward and he and the shark were inside the cavernous jaws. They closed, the light vanished and he felt himself tumbling over and over down the long neck into the interior regions of the huge creature. After he had swum around for a long time he felt the water ebbing from round him and he grounded on what seemed to be a sandbank. He could hear the shark thrashing in its death-throes close by as it suffocated in the horrid-smelling air, then suddenly all was still save for an ominous distant gurgling.

When he had rested a little, Benalli sat up and felt gingerly around with the shaft of his spear. He seemed to be in an echoing, ribbed cavern. The dead shark lay close by with many other fishes that had been engulfed.

'Well, it's a fine mess you've got us into, great-great-granduncle,' grumbled Benalli.

There was a thin chuckle from nearby in the dark, and an old man's voice said, 'At least it's peaceful enough. Here I won't have to work all the time showing stupid hunters where to find game and fish, where the wallabies are feeding and where the mullet are running.'

'Life will get dull after a time,' said Benalli cunningly.

The chuckle came again. 'I don't mind. I've done well for you, too, little great-great-nephew. Narran won't be able to find you here and turn you into a whelk so you have to eat mud the rest of your days.'

Benalli thought things over. He didn't feel clever or good looking any more. The more he thought how silly he had been the more he wanted to kick himself, though he didn't try to do that in the dark. He thought he had better consider things harder than he had ever done in his whole life if he was to escape from his plight with his life. After a time he grew hungry, so he took the sharp flint knife he carried behind the woven armlet on his left arm, and began to slice away at the tough skin of the shark's belly.

At last he got it open, and working by feel in the sloshing dark he found the second fish, which he also opened. From it he took the very first fish of all. He began slicing delicately at its belly.

'What are you doing?' roared the ghost.

'I'm hungry and I'm just getting something to chew while I wait for something else to happen,' said the young man. His fingers closed on the leather bag. He took it from the fish and hung it safely from his neck by the thong. Then he ate a fillet of the fish, quietly and slowly, for he had an idea. When he had finished he wiped his hands in his wet mop of hair, and heaved a sigh.

'What a pity!' he said, and sighed deeply again.

'What's a pity?' asked the ghost.

'No honey to finish up with,' said Benalli cunningly. Narran had said the ghost liked honey.

There was no reply, so Benalli went on, 'There's a great big enormous honeycomb in the hollow branch of a tree near my camp.' There was silence,

Many Kinds of Magic

as though the ghost was waiting for him to go on.

'The bees must have been filling it for years. There's so much in there it's running out of a crack and down the underside of the branch. I'm sorry I saved it for so long and didn't eat it. It was the pale honey, too; that's so much nicer than the dark stuff.'

There was silence in the darkness underneath the cavernous ribs, except for the ominous gurgling noise.

'Where did you say it was?' asked the ghost, finally.

'What? Oh, the honey. In that high ironbark tree near my camp. It won't be wasted, I suppose. Someone else will find it all right. Maybe someone else is looking at it right this minute. Maybe he is taking his axe and cutting into the wood while the pale honey is dripping sweetly down into the bowl he has waiting.'

The ghost was silent again.

After a while Benalli said, 'There's no trees or bees inside a Moha-moha. Just think, no more honey, ever again.'

Nobody said anything for a while and the sloshing sound went on in the background.

'I could have made some dishes of paperbark and filled them to the brim. I would have taken some back to the camp for Narran, of course. He loves the sweet stuff as much as I do. Maybe he would have shared some with his relatives . . .'

'The pale kind? That sort that is almost transparent, did you say?' asked the ghost greedily.

'That's the kind.'

Next moment Benalli was almost turned over on his back as the Moha-moha began swimming somewhere very fast. After a while there was a grating sound from beneath them, and in the distance Benalli saw an opening like the mouth of a cave seen from deep within. He picked up his spear and ran, coming out at last into the blinding sunlight on the white beach not far from his camp. He looked at the white foam on the breakers, the waving trees in the sea-wind and the loom of the many-coloured dunes, and was glad deep in his heart to be safely back in his own country. The Moha-moha shook its head in a dazed way, and reversed into the water and swam off into the blue distance.

'Did you do that?' Benalli asked Great-grand-father's ghost.

'Yes!' said the ghost absentmindedly. 'Now, about this honey. Where did you say it was?'

When Narran came back from the bunya feast Benalli handed back the little leather bag. Narran looked shrewdly at him. He seemed to be different from the young man who had waved goodbye to him so discontentedly. 'Did you have any trouble?' asked the old man.

'No trouble Uncle. I have made friends with the ghost of great-great-granduncle, too. He says he doesn't mind how often you leave him with me.'

Narran looked at the bag and at his nephew. 'This has been in the salt water and it's all sticky with honey,' he said.

'Oh, I found a bee's nest. There's two coolamons of it at your camp.'

'For me?' asked Narran, grinning.

'Of course. You might like to share some of it with your friends,' smiled Benalli.

Many Kinds of Magic

'I think,' said his uncle slowly, 'I think you might be ready now to really begin learning to be a clever fellow!'

B EARSKIN

There was once a man named Einar who escaped after the Jomsvikings were beaten at the Battle of Jorundsfjord. He put his household into his longship and fled for safety to Greenland where he settled and made a new life far from the troubles and wars of the Baltic Sea. He had a beautiful daughter named Anna who was very proud. When she had reached the age when she might be expected to marry, many of the young men came to court her.

They would come to her father's house and compete with each other at running and leaping, at weapon skill and hunting skill. She was vain and proud and would not choose among them. At last they became bitter and fought among themselves. Two of them who had been weapon-brothers in former times almost killed each other, yet still she would not make a choice.

The parents of the young men came to Einar and complained about the trouble she was causing and he spoke to her. 'What is the matter with you. Because your mother died long ago I have been easy with you and have not found a husband for you. I thought it kinder to let you choose one for yourself. Now this trouble has come with our neighbours, and still you will not choose a man and end the fighting.'

Anna tossed her gold hair disdainfully and said, 'Both these young men say they love me, yet after they fought, both are still alive. If either had really loved me then he would be dead or his rival would be dead. I will not choose.'

'Then I will choose a husband for you and that will be the end of it,' said Einar grimly and sent her away to work in the kitchen.

Next evening when the young men gathered as usual there came also a tall man cloaked in the skin of a white bear. He wore the bear's head above his helmet and his dark face peered through the open mouth and past the terrible teeth. When the young men invited him to join in their sports, he laid aside the polar-bear cloak and joined them on the exercise field. He was enormously strong and agile. He twirled the heavy blunt iron practice-sword as though it was a twig of wood and drubbed all who came against him. While they nursed their bruised heads and ribs he cast his spear far and truly, and when he took up his bow, his arrows found the gold of the target almost every time.

Einar was watching the stranger, and said he looked like a proper warrior, and called him to share the ale-cup with him. The young men drew together and murmured when they saw Einar's white locks close to the dark hair of the stranger as they talked. They suspected Bearskin was asking for Anna for a wife but none there was brave enough to challenge him.

Next morning Einar called Anna to him and said, 'I have given you to Bearskin for wife. He asks no dowry, having plenty of silver of his own, but I will give him the smaller boat, which is sound, and I give you the chest of clothing that was your mother's.'

Anna protested, but her father said, 'I am tired of your pride. You wanted a fighter, I have found one for you. Life here will be quieter when you have gone. When a man has been on the losing side in a great battle and is growing old he wants peace in his hall, not brawling. Bearskin can keep the peace in his own hall, and from what I have seen of him he is able to do that. You have a husband, be content!'

She wept and lamented but it did her no good. When he was ready to leave, Bearskin took her under one arm and her chest under the other and carried her to the boat. She kicked and bit and fought but he managed her easily enough, and dumped her in the stern. When she would have leapt ashore again he simply growled, 'Sit still or I will bind you to the seat!' A rough husband he turned out to be! He loosed the painter and thrust the boat out on to the waves as if it was a toy. He unfurled and set the square sail and took the steering oar. The wind carried them out to sea, and he pointed the bows north toward the grey wastes of water leading to the ice. Anna wailed all the way till at last her husband said impatiently, 'Quiet woman. Your crying will bring the whales and the dragons of the deep and they will swallow you!'

After that she was silent, though she muttered,

'That might be an easier fate for me than this marriage!'

All that day and the night that followed they sailed north along the desolate coast. Sleet blew and froze on them, hail fell like the blows of dwarf's hammers and the wind and sea lifted in a tempest but Bearskin handled the boat with ease and skill and seemed not to notice the weather. He even sang songs of the whalepath they followed, deep chants of the men who live by the sea. When dawn lit the grey water he took dried fish and bread from a locker and offered it to Anna with fresh water to drink. She tasted them and spat but he only said, 'That is the fare we have till we reach my home; you may eat it or not as you wish,' and went on tending sail and oar.

About noon they passed some low skerries of rock just breaking the surface of the ocean. These were landmarks of some kind, for Bearskin lowered sail and took the oars. He rowed tirelessly, his brawny arms bending the looms of the oars as his strong strokes drove the boat through the water. By evening they were travelling between two long, low promontories where gulls screamed about their heads. Twice, Anna saw seals slip from the rocky shore into the water as the boat slid by.

At length they hauled alongside a small jetty built from thick pine logs and sheltered from the waves by a jut of black stone. Bearskin made the painter fast to a bollard, and stepped ashore, arranging his long white cloak of skin around him. He took the chest of clothes under one arm and his weapons in his free hand and strode off along a faint path

Many Kinds of Magic

through the rounded black boulders. Anna had to scramble out unaided and stumble after her rough husband. At first her pride forbade her to hurry but when he began to draw distant from her she looked around at the grey sky, the black stones and cold sea and hated to be left alone in such a place. Though she felt no love for Bearskin yet there was no other company or comfort and she felt safe where he was, so grim was he. He was grim as the land itself, and she hurried a little and caught him up.

She clung to the back of his white cloak as they climbed the last steep pinch to the entrance of a cavern high on the slope of a bare hill overlooking the long gulf of tide-torn water and blowing wind.

'This is our home, wife,' said the man. 'Here will we have our wedding feast. Go in and start the fire and cook the food. I'll go and bid the guests to our celebration, for I have a few companions hereabouts, though none have wives.'

He made ready to leave, but she stopped him. 'Whoever heard of a bride to cook her own wedding feast?' she asked indignantly.

'It is the custom among your people, and I thought you might want to follow it,' he said patiently. 'You are the only one here who can do it, for as I said, my fellows are all single and have no wives. I cannot cook anything myself, for food to me is but fuel for my body, be it cooked or raw. It is all one to me whether we have this feast or not, though perhaps it would be better for both of us if we did. If you wish it we will have it; if you do not, then we will not bother. You must choose for yourself.'

'I will not have such a feast!' said Anna proudly.

'You have chosen for the first time,' said Bearskin sadly.

Anna found when she entered the cave that though the housing might be rough she had no reason to complain of her husband's poverty. There were barrels of good ale, chests of barley meal and oats, dried turnips in plenty and huge sides of smoked beef and pork and salmon. The cave was floored with white sand where it was not laid with the spray-whitened timbers of old ships. There was plenty of sweet hay and warm wool blankets in the box-beds along the walls and when her husband took a key from his neck-chain and unlocked a great chest to put away his golden armbands she saw the glint of gold and the pale moon-colour of silver before he closed it again.

She started a fire and cooked them a meal. Her husband ate heartily. By the time they ended eating night was falling outside. Bearskin took up his cloak and said, 'I must be about my business. Do not go outside the cave for any reason. There are fierce wolf packs and hungry bears roam hereabouts, they would swallow you in two gulps. None dare enter here where I am master, for they fear me; but outside is no man's land and they would be swift to seize you.'

'Where are you going?' she asked nervously.

'To follow the thing Fate has given me to do,' he replied. 'Remember, do not leave the hearth or the cave no matter what you might hear or you will not live long to regret it. But the choice is yours to make.' With that he walked away, a huge shaggy shape with his broad-axe thrust through his wide leather belt and his great spear in his hand.

When he had gone silently in his soft skin boots Anna sat on a block of wood by the hearth and wept. She had been too proud to show her sorrow while he was there but now she was alone with her grief. There was no sound but the crackle of the driftwood fire where little tongues of blue, green and yellow flame ran along the wood above the white ash. When Anna had done with her bitter tears she rose and cleared away the meal, being too proud to give her husband cause to say she did not know what was due to her position and dignity. Then she crept silently to the mouth of the cavern and peered out over the bleak hillside through the gloaming.

There was naught to see save sea and sky and stone, naught to hear save water and cold wind and now and then a gull crying. A sad note, that was.

Then, faint and faraway she heard the wail of a wolf pack on the trail of their prey and from closer to hand the sound as of bears roaring in combat. Anna shivered and was about to return to the fire when from the skerries below by the stony shore she heard sweet music blown on the wind. The music was of piping and drumming and along with these sweet sounds she thought she heard the voices of men and women talking and singing and laughing. In the sky to the north was a great wave of leaping fire like dancers, and the colour and grandeur of the fire seemed to wax and fade as the music rose and fell. She watched and listened entranced until there came a terrifying roar from the shores of the sea, a series of loud splashes, and then the music was heard no more. She shivered with chill and ran in to the fire, feeding it with wood till it blazed higher and comforted her.

She sat late while the stars wheeled half across the heavens but her husband did not return. Worn out at last by hard travelling and a hard fate she crept into one of the warm beds and slept till daylight brought the sounds of her man stirring outside.

So began a new life for Anna. She saw no one but her husband save when sometimes he brought home another of his kind, huge and shaggy and wrapped in polar-bear hide to drink ale with him beside the hearth during the long evenings of summer. Even when she handed them the ale-horn or great platters of food these men did not speak or even look at her. Once she almost struck one in her rage at being thus ignored, but the man turned such terrible eyes toward her that her desperate rage turned to fear and she fled away. Every night Bearskin went on his mysterious errands leaving her alone, and she was always asleep when he returned. Sometimes she found new stores of food among the supplies and knew he must have brought them, but he never mentioned it and would not reply when she asked him about it.

At last came Midsummer Eve, and it was the time of longest light and shortest dark in the year. Anna could not sleep. She felt no drowsiness. When Bearskin had gone she went to the mouth of the cavern and sat to watch the path of the sun across the water where it was just dipped below the horizon. For once the wind had stopped its eternal wailing among the rocky crags and the sky was clear of cloud.

All was silent, such a stillness as she had not known

Many Kinds of Magic

before in that grim place. Even the wolves and bears were quiet. A ghostly silver light glimmered on water and land so all seemed softer than ever before. Suddenly Anna heard again the sound of wild music from the strand and the cheerful calling of merry voices as men and women rejoiced in dancing and singing.

'Now is my chance for a little mirth, the first I have known since I came to this dreary place,' thought Anna. 'These sound to be gentle happy folk. I will go and look at them secretly and if they be rough I can steal away back to safety here, and Bearskin will never know I have chosen to disobey him.'

She slipped from the cave and downhill toward the sounds of music and laughter. When she got close to the beach she hid in the black shadow of a huge boulder looming over the little sandy cover. From its shelter she cautiously raised her head and eyes till she could see over the flinty top. Her eyes widened in amazement.

Under the seaward side of the rock, just below her, were five pipers puffing and fingering as they trolled the melody forth, while a sixth musician beat sturdily on a little skin drum. Close by on the sand were men and women, their naked bodies shining silver in the glow of the midnight sun. They wove in an intricate dance by the rippling water, keeping perfect time to the melody as they danced in chains and patterns on the sand. They were all young; the men strong and nimble and the women supple and graceful. It was a happy scene.

Anna was so caught up in wonder at the sight

of the graceful dancing she forgot to be cautious. She raised her head from the shadow of the stone and the light glinted gold on her long fair hair. This bright flicker caught the eye of one of the men and in an instant he had run to the rock and pulled her roughly from her hiding-place. The music stopped abruptly in mid-note, and the dancers and players gathered quickly round her, pinching and jostling her and tugging roughly at her hair and clothes.

'Bear! Bear! She smells of bear!' screamed one woman. The others took up the cry of 'Bear Woman!', scratching her cheeks and tearing at her until she screamed with rage and fear and pain. She began to fight them off, but though she was strong and tall and well made these folk mastered her easily. Soon she was led panting and weeping to where their chieftain stood. Held from behind by both arms and her long hair cruelly pulled back, she was forced to meet the eyes of the leader.

'Bearwoman?' he said thoughtfully. 'Indeed she smells of our enemies but I think there is more to her than that. You now; are you a woman of our enemies?'

'I am Anna Einarsdotter, wife of the chieftain Bearskin, and he will call you to account for any hurt you do to me,' she said proudly through bruised lips.

'So, you are human, though wedded to the chief of our enemies,' he said thoughtfully. He turned to the others. 'We will not kill her straight away for her spying, then. She shall be slave to the Selkies until she dies, and that will hurt him in his heart when he discovers it, knowing his wife is subject to his enemies. How sweet it is to bring sorrow to the one who has oppressed us for so long.'

The pipers sounded a triumphant noise of music at this, and the drummer beat a slow roll on the taut skin of his drum.

'Come, children, the dancing is over and we will go home,' said the leader of the Selkies. Some held her fast while others ran to what Anna had thought to be their garments piled on the rocks. To her horror she now saw that these were not clothing but sealskins and as soon as the people slipped them on they were transformed into seals, grey seals with long whiskers and great round eyes. When all had changed they began to drag her into the cold grey water.

'I will drown, I will drown!' she screamed, but the biggest seal tied a charm roughly around her wrist where it clung and burned like fire. When at last they forced her head below the surface she found she could breathe easily enough. She made a last despairing effort to break free and as her head broke the moon-mirror of the surface for the last time she saw an enormous white bear rushing toward the shore, bellowing in grief and anger. Then she was forced below and down so she no longer saw the strand but only the darkness of deep water and the little fishes swimming through the fronds of the long ribbons of brown weed that swayed in the send of the sea.

Now began a time of great suffering and sorrow for Anna for she was slave and servant to all the Selkies, and any who wished to beat her might do so. She was set to long tasks with little food and less rest. The charm around her wrist burned like a constant fire and she could not wrench it free for all her trying. She learned from things said to her in scorn that the bears and seals had been foes for many generations, and that her husband, though seeming to be a man, was really chieftain of the white bears and one of their most feared warriors. The Selkies hated him for his bravery and skill and delighted to use her spitefully for hurts he had done their people in years gone by.

Many times she thought of escape but the charm clasped to her wrist could only be removed by magic so they did not need to watch her closely. Sometimes she would steal away for a time to a rough little island surrounded by the wild sea and there she could creep from the water on to the dry rock to weep for her present misery.

As the time went by Anna began to think of her marriage to Bearskin as having been a time of joy. She had been lonely but her man had guarded her and looked to her well being, rough though he might have been. She remembered Bearskin with affection and this slowly turned to love. She was sure that the bear who had charged so recklessly and vainly to her rescue must have been her husband. She felt his roaring had been as much for grief at her plight as anger at his foes. She wished heartily again and again she had done as he advised and not left the safety of their home.

One day as she sat on the hard stone of the island bewailing her fate she saw a twisted bush growing in a crevice in the rock. Its twigs were misshapen by the constant wind and its roots thirsted for kindly rain; it was a poor-looking, dry thing, yet from the end of one branch hung a small, exquisite blossom. Anna was overwhelmed.

'I have complained of my fate, and now I am ashamed,' she said aloud. 'Yours has been a harder fate than mine, I think, here in this salty desolation. Yet you have love and trust and faith, and you blossom in the wilderness though none would ever know it, save by accident. Your courage is greater than mine.'

Saying which, she wept for the sake of the bravery of the bush. Her tears fell on the dry soil at the base of the stem where the roots clung to the rock and sandy earth. At once a soft music sounded in the air around Anna. The tree began to grow and spread until it stood tall above her and its branches spread in a canopy over her chilled body. It dropped golden leaves to carpet the hard rock and the fragrance of its flower that burst from the twigs surrounded Anna like a blessing. From across the sea a golden bird came and settled on a branch above her, singing so sweetly she wept again for joy at the beauty of its voice. A tear fell on the charm that burned on her wrist so it withered and fell from her.

The Selkies, feeling the vanishment of their enchantment as it fell away came to try to capture Anna once more, but the tree spread its protection over her and they could not come beneath it. Anna huddled in the shelter and to her astonishment the bird spoke.

'Your pride brought you to this, now your love has freed you a little. Remember your thoughts of exile when you are once more restored to what you had, for in that way lies more than your own salvation.'

At that moment Anna saw a distant speck on the far horizon of water and as she watched she saw it was Bearskin coming toward the island rowing the boat as mightily as he was able. At sight of him the seals vanished below the waves, and as the prow grated on the gravelly beach the bird took wing and flew off.

With a glad cry she ran to the waterside and tumbled headlong aboard. Bearskin spoke no word of reproof or happiness as she clung to his rough cloak and hard body. Gently he set her on the seat, spun the little boat around and hoisted sail, for the wind was fair for their course. He brought her safely back to the cave she now looked upon as her home. It was late Autumn and the days of long Winter dark were coming fast. Still Bearskin said no word at all, and when she begged him to speak he only smiled and made a sign that he was forbidden to do so. Yet it was the first time she had seen him smile and she was content.

Through the long winter night he mostly slept, as was the custom of his people, though he would waken now and then to walk the bounds he had set around his home to make sure none had intruded. Then he would sleep again. Anna waited his waking with patience, smiling, speaking kindly to him and expecting no reply. In the Spring of the year she bore him a son while he was away on his restless patrolling. When she handed him the boy on his return he was so overjoyed she thought he might speak but he said no word, just nursed the child gently and she knew he loved it. After the child was born she was never alone again and a quiet happiness grew in her, though sometimes she wished she might return to her people for a visit to show them her new son.

When a year had passed from the time that Bearskin had rescued her from the island, Bearskin was sitting with the child on his knee when he said to her, 'The time is ended for me to be silent. Now, Anna, proud Anna, is the time for you to make your third choice. I offered a wedding feast and you chose your pride. I offered you safety and your pride drove you to captivity. Now I offer you a third choice, the last of all. If you wish you may go home to your father's house where he will welcome you, for the sake of his grandson if for no other reason. If you choose this, I will release you from your marriage to find what happiness you may with some other man who is gentler and kinder than I am. Or you may choose to stay here to the end of your days with me if that is what you want. Think well before you choose, for it is the last choice I have to offer you. I am going about my business now. You can tell me your choice when I return.'

He stepped from the cave and vanished. It was late afternoon when he returned. He found Anna cooking his meal as usual with the baby sleeping on a blanket beside the fire.

'Have you decided?' He did not look at her when he spoke.

'This is my home and you are my husband and that is our son,' said Anna calmly. 'Here are we three together, and here will I stay with you both until I die, if you will let me.'

At her words Bearskin took her in his strong arms and suddenly his rough looks and airs vanished leaving him as tall and fair and straight a man as any who walked the earth.

'The spell is broken, the spell is broken!' he shouted, kissing Anna.

'What spell, husband?' she asked wonderingly.

'It was a curse laid on me by a wicked old woman,' said Bearskin. 'I am the son of a chieftain of the Danes. I was hunting alone one day when I killed a deer, not knowing it was her pet and familiar. "You are too proud!" she screeched. "Rough and uncouth you will be, and living in a far icy place until you marry the proudest woman in the world. She alone can break the spell. Three choices only can you give her, and unless she chooses to stay with you then you will stay in this shape till the world runs down!" Then she pointed her skinny finger at me and I became as you have always seen me. Now the curse is ended, for you have freed us both. Now I can say farewell to my hairy brothers and live as a man again until I die.'

He picked up his son and embraced her and the child both at the same time. Not long after they left the bleak shores of Bear Island and returned to the lands of living men, and there they are living still if they have not died by now.

UGONG WOMAN

Once long ago on an island in the waters of the Sea Of Coral there lived a beautiful young woman on the Island Of Warriors. Her name was Gizarri and she was a *Wakuniaingawakaz*. That means she was a 'mat-stay-girl'; one who must not do any work. They are chosen for their beauty, and all they have to do is stay on their mat and look beautiful, so all the people may come to see them and admire them.

Every morning Gizarri walked to the beach of white coral sand to swim, to wash herself and to wash her skirts and hang them to dry on the bushes in the steady south-east wind of the Dry Season. On her way home to the village she would gather lovely flowers and coloured seeds. When she returned, her mother and sisters would rub her body gently with coconut oil and decorate her with the blossoms she had brought. Her grandmother would make armlets and necklaces from the coloured seeds and put them on her. Then she would sit on her mat and people going by would see her and admire her. Gizarri was gentle and kind and so she never became vain as some mat-stay-girls do.

One morning she went to the beach as usual. She washed her skirts and hung them to dry, then she bathed in the warm salt water that lay calm and shallow behind the shelter of the coral reef. Then she lay in the water; half dreaming as she listened to the sounds of the south-east wind gently stirring the branches, the hushing of wavelets and the tiny tinkle of the water stirring the fragments of broken coral so they sounded like tiny bells.

She heard a splashing in the lagoon out by the reef. When she raised her head to look, she saw it was a beautiful young man diving and swimming in the deeper water just inside the coral barrier. He was the finest swimmer Gizarri had ever seen. He spent almost all his time under the surface and came up to breathe only occasionally. His body was sturdy and strong. She waited until he was facing her way, then she moved so he would notice her. She had fallen in love with him and wanted him to be her husband. Yet he seemed very shy. He just waved to her a little, then dived under the surface and she didn't see him any more though she waited for a long time. So she took her dried washing and went home.

Next morning Gizarri found a beautiful pearl-shell ornament on the beach at her usual swimming place. She guessed it was a gift from the shy young man so she put it on and wore it. When she had finished bathing and was lying in the shallows he came again, swimming along the inside edge of the reef as he had done the day before. He came closer this day but he would not come too near nor would he answer when she called softly to him. He seemed so shy although he was so tall and strong! She rose and began wading through the warm, shallow, transparent water toward him but he saw her coming and slipped under the surface again and she saw him no more that day, so after a while she went home. On the way she hid the pearl-shell ornament for fear her relatives would ask her where she got it and she didn't want to tell because they would chase the young man away.

That night as she lay on her soft sleeping mat, listening to the hushing and rattling of the warm breeze fanning the dead palm branches she began to wonder where the good-looking young man came from. She knew he did not come from her own Island of Warriors. Perhaps if she got to the beach early enough she would be able to see him arrive! Then she might have an idea where he lived, and which house he came from. Perhaps he was from one of the other islands and was visiting relatives.

She was early at the sheltered beach next morning. She hid herself and waited. To her surprise, no one came along the beach or over the hill. Then her eye was caught by a movement out to sea, and a big dugong came in from the dark-blue waters outside the reef. It swam through the shallows and to the beach. Then she saw a wonder – the dugong took off its skin and out stepped the young man she loved. He hid in the cover of a fig tree standing close to the beach where he could secretly watch the path from the village along which she usually came. Gizarri knew he was waiting to see her. She was excited because now she knew that he must love her, too.

She crept around palms and hid in the bushes and slipped carefully through the undergrowth till she was out of his sight. Then she rose, and walked along the path to the beach, singing softly so he would know she was coming. She sang:

> He is beautiful, he is straight and strong
> This young man from the sea.
> He is braver and stronger than any of the young
>   men
> From the hills and the beaches!

She knew he was listening and would know she loved him.

Turning her back to the wild fig tree she began to wash the skirts she carried. She didn't look up when she heard the sound of his feet in the sand – *swish-swish-swish* – as he came toward her. When he spoke she pretended to be surprised.

'I would like to talk to you this morning,' he said. 'I have been waiting to make sure you wouldn't mind. I don't want people to think I'm a rude person who doesn't know his manners. I heard your song as you came along, and so I thought you wouldn't mind.'

'I don't mind if we talk a little,' said Gizarri shyly. 'I wanted to thank you for the ornament; it is beautiful.'

'Why aren't you wearing it?'

'I haven't told my people about you,' she confessed. 'My father and two brothers are fierce warriors. They might kill you if they found you had been talking to me, because I am a mat-stay-girl and they will arrange for the young men to dance before me when they think it is time for me to choose a husband.'

The young man frowned. He could do the dances of the sea, but he did not know the dances of the land. 'I must not stray from out of the sound of the water or I will die,' he said.

'Then you wouldn't be able to join the dancers, and so I cannot choose you and you cannot claim me,' said Gizarri sadly.

'Will you marry me and come into the sea with me, then?'

'I can't live in the water all the time. I would drown and die. Yet I want to be your wife,' said Gizarri simply.

'Then go and fetch the ornament I gave you. Put it on and come back here. It is mother-of-pearl, it is magic. When you wear it you can live in the water all the time. I will go and get a skin for you. I am a young man of the Dugong People, the people who live in the sea and harm no one. Put on the skin I bring and I will put on mine, and wear the charm. Then we can be husband and wife and live in the water with my people.'

Gizarri wept, for she loved her family and friends, but her love for the young man was so great. She walked slowly along the path and got the ornament from its hiding-place and put it on. As she returned she sang:

> *I am sad to leave my mother - o - o,*
> *I am sad to leave my father and my family.*
> *Goodbye hills and trees and white beach,*
> *Goodbye air and the trees that wave in you.*
> *I am sad to leave you, grandmother - o - o,*

I am going with my husband, the young man I love,
I am going to the water - o - o,
I will be a dugong.

She came to the beach where her new husband waited for her with a dugong skin. She slipped the pearl-shell ornament over her head and made sure it was secure, and then put on the dugong skin. So did he, and next minute there were no more people on the beach; just two sleek young dugong swimming strongly toward the open sea beyond the reef and the broad shallow places where the turtle-grass grows, there to find his people and join them.

When Gizarri did not return from the beach at her usual time her grandmother and her sisters went to find her. They found the clean skirts dried on the bushes but the tide had returned and wiped away all footprints from the sand. There were only the clothes waving forlornly in the south-east wind, lonely and forsaken. Gizarri would never wear them again. The old woman and the two young ones hurried back to the village with the news that their beloved mat-stay-girl had vanished.

Oh, there was a hunt then! Her father and brothers took their weapons and looked all over the island in case some man had stolen her, but they could not find trace or tracks. Other warriors helped; firstly because Gizarri's father was a Shark Man and they were a little afraid of him, but most of all because they were angry that one of the young women had been stolen, a beautiful one, a mat-stay-girl.

When they had ended their fruitless search of

the whole island Gizarri's father said, 'It must have been raiders from the next island who came in a canoe and took her! We will raid them and bring her back and take revenge!'

Gizarri's brothers said, 'We will take heads for this insult! They scorn us, do they? We will show them who are the warriors, the fighters, the slayers! We will not rest till we have got the heads of the men who stole our sister!' They went off to prepare their weapons and to sing the death songs, the fierce, bloody songs of the Shark Men.

That night Gizarri's grieving grandmother had a dream. She dreamt she was under the water walking across a plain of emerald-green turtle-grass toward a wedding among the Dugong People. There were many of them, old grandfather and grandmother dugong, strong men and fine, plump women dugong, and many small ones. One of the handsome grand-mother dugong came to greet her and said, 'Welcome to this wedding that will make us sisters, you and me.' She took Gizarri's grandmother by the hand and led her to a place of great honour among the company. Then was led before her two youngsters, both fat and handsome, a young man and woman of the Dugong People. 'This is your new grandson, and this is my new grandaughter,' said the dugong grandmother. 'She is a dugong now because she has married my grandson and joined our people as the custom is.'

The land grandmother looked at the young couple, and she thought that though the young woman was all of the water, yet her eyes were Gizarri's eyes. She knew the one inside the skin was Gizarri. 'Ah,

Gizarri there is something I must know. Did this young man take you away by force, or did you follow him because your heart told you that you must?'

Gizarri said, 'This is my husband and this is my home now, and this was my free choice.' Then they hugged each other, the young woman in her strange form and the old woman, for on land they had loved each other dearly and this might be the last time they would meet in life.

Then the land grandmother woke up and heard the south-east wind moving in the palm branches. She saw the thatch of the hut and felt the softness of her sleeping mat under her and smelt the salt wind from the sea, and knew she had been dreaming. But her cheeks were still wet with tears, and caught between two of her toes was a piece of green turtle-grass still wet from the sea! So she knew she had discovered what was really happening, she thought she had really been to her grandaughter's wedding. She hurried and told her son-in-law what she had dreamed and showed him the blade of wet seagrass.

'Mother of my wife, grandmother of my children, if this be true then my daughter has wed a dugong man and gone away for ever,' said the father and he wept, for he loved his children dearly. 'I will not hunt dugong any more because I might kill my daughter or my grandchildren!'

But Gizarri's two brothers had sung their songs and sharpened their spears and sworn their oaths and prayed their prayers and they would not forgive their sister and her husband. 'We will hunt this dugong man and kill him; we will have our revenge for this woman-theft!' they said.

'She was not stolen, she went willingly,' said their grandmother sharply but the young men would not listen. They got the things they used for hunting dugong:

> The narapat, which marks the spot to build the
>   hunting tower.
> The parts for the naiat, the platform where the
>   hunter stands.
> The wat, the harpoon-spear to strike their prey.
> The rope called amu to bind their victim when
>   it is speared.

They put all these things in their canoes and went to the reefs and plains of turtle-grass where the dugong feed. There they searched until they found where many of the great sea creatures had been cropping the grass at high tide the night before. They knew the animals would return when the water came back, so they built the platform and made ready the cruel harpoon. One stayed on the naiat while the other paddled to the beach. So they waited for the tide to flood and their prey to return.

Gizarri knew her brothers were vengeful men. She knew they would try to get a pay-back from her husband, so she stayed with him and warned him and his people not to go to their usual undersea pasture. They all went away from the Island of Warriors to another place and stayed there for a year. When that time was gone they began to get homesick for their own place again, the country where they had lived so long. They said, 'Our hearts are sorry because we don't see our own home any more. After this time your brothers might have got tired and given up the hunt. We'll just go back and visit our old home.'

Gizarri had a child now, a fine little boy and she didn't want to take him where there might be danger. Yet her husband was homesick too, and wanted to go with his people so she went with her husband because she loved him. All the dugong went back to their own place.

When the dugong all went away Gizarri's brothers had stopped trying to hunt them. Now, one day when they were out spearing fish and diving round the reefs for crayfish the younger one saw a place where dugong had been feeding on the seagrass.

'They have come back, brother!' he shouted when he came back to the surface, to breathe and hand the crayfish to his older brother in the canoe. 'Get the narapat to mark the place, and then we'll go home and get the rest of the gear. Tonight we'll go hunting!'

They marked the place with the narapat and paddled back to the beach for the platform. They brought it back and built the hunting eyrie very strongly. There the younger brother waited in silence and stillness until it was dusk and the tide was almost at the flood. Then he heard the sound of dugong in the night, breathing in the silence of that watery, lapping place.

'Sssshhhhhhhhhh. Sssshhhhhhhhhh,' went the sound, coming nearer. It was Gizarri and her little son, coming to eat the grass. Her husband was with them. When he lifted his nose above the water to breathe he made a deeper sound: 'Ssssuhhhhhh.

Ssssuhhhhhhhhh.' Just like a deep sigh.

Younger brother waited till the sound was just below him then thrust with the harpoon, leaping with it so the weight of his body would thrust it well home. He missed Gizarri and her husband but he speared the baby. It cried, but soon it was dead. Younger brother climbed back on to the naiat and pulled the body in with the rope amu. He could lift the body up to the platform with him because it was so small. He knew the parents would not go away. They would be sorry to lose their baby, so they would stay and he might catch them, too.

Sure enough, in a little while he heard the sound of the husband dugong again, coming closer. 'Ssssuhhhh. Ssssuhhhhhhhh.' When it was below him, looking for the baby, he leapt out and thrust the harpoon down. This time he speared the husband. The husband struggled strongly, but the rope held and at last he tangled himself in it so he could not rise to breathe, and he drowned.

Gizarri wept. Younger brother climbed back on to the naiat and waited for morning to come with the canoe and his big brother to help. He could not lift the husband dugong on to the platform; he was too heavy.

Gizarri took off the dugong skin she had worn for so long and let it drift away. She swam to the naiat and shouted in her human voice, 'You have murdered your nephew and your brother-in-law! You have killed the people I love most. Now I will follow them to the Place Of The Dead, but before I go I will curse you, little brother, for your great pride and cruelty and anger!' Then she cursed him with strong curses. She took the ornament from round her neck that let her live safely in the deeps and flung it from her. Then she swam off and vanished.

When day dawned older brother came in the canoe to see what luck little brother might have had in the darkness. There was no sign of little brother any more! Only where the naiat had stood was a black pillar of rock. Close by three more new rocks broke the smooth surface of the sea. One was like a big man dugong, the others were the same as a mother dugong with her baby swimming beside her.

These rocks are still there and people say that sometimes the Dugong People come there and cry for Gizarri and her family. They will never be forgotten.